RENDEZVOUS WITH DEATH

"Wait for me here," said Ben Kane.

Franklin Smith waited, wondering what the sheriff was up to. It had to have something to do with the investigation of the murders of the prostitutes.

Kane returned driving a buggy. "Climb in," he said. Smith got in, and Kane drove down the backstreet and out of town.

"Sheriff," said Smith, "Where are we going?"

"You'll see soon enough," said Kane.

Smith looked back over his shoulder and saw the town getting smaller and smaller behind him.

"If you're looking for a private place to talk," he said, "I think we've gone far enough."

"Not quite," said Kane. He finally turned off the road and headed down into a creek bed. In the middle of the creek, he stopped.

"What the hell are you up to?" said Smith.

"You couldn't take my advice, could you?" Kane said, his eyes narrowing. "You had to keep poking around in it."

"But sheriff—"

"Shut up!" Kane said, and turning in his seat he unbuttoned his coat to reveal a 1878 model Colt .45 with a short four-inch barrel that shone in the sunlight . . .

TEXAS NOOSE

JAKE FOSTER

ZEBRA BOOKS
KENSINGTON PUBLISHING CORP.

ZEBRA BOOKS

are published by

Kensington Publishing Corp.
475 Park Avenue South
New York, NY 10016

First printing: December, 1990

Printed in the United States of America

Chapter One

Ellie McKee sat stiff and proud in the passenger car as the train raced south. It was her first ride on a railroad, and she traveled with a sense of adventure, in spite of the urgency of her mission. Even so, it was a tiring journey. She had known that it would be a long trip, but she had not quite anticipated the sense of endlessness that would accompany it, the feeling that she had always been moving and that she would continue moving forever. Of course, she knew that was not the case. She knew exactly how long she had been away from home, and she knew how much more time would be required to finish the journey. Still there was the feeling of endlessness.

In fact the conductor had just a few moments earlier come through the car with his announcement that they would soon be at the end of the line. That would not be the end of Ellie's journey, however. It would mark the beginning of the last leg. The tracks did not go as far as Ellie needed to go, so she would ride the rails as far as possible and then travel the rest of the way by stagecoach. It seemed strange to Ellie, with the world moving into the twentieth century, that she would not be able to complete her trip by rail. It was possible to circle entirely by rail the place she was going, but there was still a vast expanse of Texas inside that giant circle where no rails had been laid. In areas like that, she knew, the not quite obsolete stage lines still filled the need. They even maintained a few short runs into somewhat remote regions of her native Kansas. And after all, she had begun the trip on horseback. Partly to make the time seem to pass faster, she thought back over the last few months of her short life, considering the events that had brought her to this point.

The first nineteen years of Ellie's life had been carefree and happy. One might even say, she admitted only to herself, that she had been spoiled by doting parents. She was an only child, and she had come late in the lives of her parents. They had fussed over her and coddled her. They had given her, so far as was possible for them, everything she ever wanted. But they had not been overly protective. They had allowed her to run free, and she had grown up with the entire two-thousand acre ranch as her playground. She had learned to ride and rope and shoot with the best of the cowhands who worked for her father, J.W. McKee.

And the cowhands, too, had all treated her like a princess. J.W. was the king, Mollie the queen and Ellie the princess. But none of the boys had ever tried to court her. They didn't dare. They knew, without its ever being stated in so many words, that she was somehow above them. There had been plenty of times when Ellie had wished that they didn't feel that way, that the invisible but still very real gap between them did not exist. She hardly knew any other eligible males. Oh, there had been Clarence Dibble, the banker's boy, who had lately taken to riding around the countryside in that ridiculous gas buggy his father had purchased, but Ellie could out-ride, out-rope, out-shoot, out-wrestle and probably out-box him. And there had been Amos Jones, the young school teacher. He had actually come calling once, but he was a pompous ass, and he was an Eastern dude. Ellie had not found him to be much more interesting than Clarence. The only other one that had seemed like a real possibility had been Dalton Bradley. Dalton's father, old William Byrd Bradley, owned the other large ranch in the valley. That meant, of course, that she and Dalton were on an equal social level, and folks just thought it natural that Dalton should pursue her. But she had always thought that Dalton was just too stuck on himself. He thought that he was God's gift to women, and he thought that women should recognize that in him as clearly as he recognized it himself. He had once asked her to go riding with him on a Saturday night, but she had known what he wanted all right, and she had told him just where he could go in no uncertain terms.

That had been the only problem with life on the ranch, and, of course, it had not been a real problem until the last few years. When she had been younger, the attention of her parents and of all the cowhands on the ranch had been more than enough for Ellie. That had all changed in recent years. She had begun to be aggravated with the fact that the only single men around who dared to approach her were young twits. She had begun to wish that some of the cowboys had more spunk. And then, just three months ago, Richard Fuller had come to town. Ellie had gone to town with her mother to do some shopping. One of the cowboys had driven them in the buckboard. And Ellie had seen him walking down the sidewalk. He was a handsome devil, she recalled. He couldn't possibly have been thirty years old yet. But he did sport a nice, thin mustache, and he was dressed, oh, so well. She remembered clearly her first reaction to the man.

"Who's that stranger there?" she had said.

Her mother gave him a quick glance, then looked away as quickly.

"He has the look of a riverboat gambler," she said. "I can't imagine what he's doing out here on the prairie."

Ellie did not say any more about him, but she continued to watch him as he walked down the sidewalk. Then he went into the saloon, and Ellie figured that her mother had been at least half right about the man. He probably was a gambler, and he was probably going into the saloon to ply his trade. The rest of the day was uneventful. Even the shopping was boring. But that Friday night there was a dance in town, and Ellie went. J.W. and Mollie went too, and it was while the king and queen were out on the floor dancing with each other that the princess was approached by the handsome stranger.

"Hello," he said. "May I have this dance?"

"I've been taught not to dance with strangers," Ellie said, but her smile told the stranger that she was being coy. She intended that it would.

"Excuse me," he said, and he turned and walked away, and Ellie felt like a fool. She wanted to dance with him, wanted to get to know him, and she responded to his request the way she knew her mother would want her to respond, but with the added smile, and so he was gone. Then Dalton Bradley approached her and asked for a dance and she couldn't think of a good reason to refuse, so she danced with

8

him. When the music stopped, he asked her to go outside with him.

"Whatever for?" she said, and she turned to walk away. She almost walked right into the stranger. He was standing there with Clarence Dibble.

"Oh," she said. "Excuse me."

The stranger gouged Clarence in the ribs.

"Uh, Ellie," Clarence said, "I'd like you to meet Mr. Richard Fuller. Mr. Fuller, this is Ellie McKee."

Ellie smiled and looked Fuller directly in the eyes.

"How do you do, Mr. Fuller," she said.

Fuller bowed graciously.

"It's a pleasure to meet you," he said, and then the band started to play another tune. "May I have this dance?"

"Well, yes," she said, and they danced the rest of the night, and it was wonderful. Later she realized that she had learned very little about Richard Fuller during that time. They had danced almost every dance together, and the few dances they skipped, they spent talking. He told her that his profession was gambling, and he said something about Deadwood, South Dakota. Her impression was that he had come to Kansas from there. South Dakota seemed a long ways off, almost like a foreign country, and Ellie thought that she would like to travel, to get away from the ranch and from Kansas, at least for a little while, but not to South Dakota, to some big city perhaps, San Francisco or New Orleans or Chicago. Those places were probably filled with gamblers and with naughty ladies. Probably everyone had telephones and those silly horseless carriages. Richard Fuller had undoubtedly seen all of that. And more. She had no idea where he came from originally or what kind of family he came from, the things her mother would have wanted to

9

know. But that didn't bother her at all. She left the dance feeling as if she had just spent the most beautiful evening of her entire life. She really felt like a princess.

But life has a way of balancing out extremes, and when the McKees got home that evening, they also had the first big fight of their lives. Staring out the window of the speeding train, Ellie recalled the incident with sadness, and a tear ran down her cheek. She opened her purse, took out from under the British Webley Bulldog revolver J.W. bought her for her last birthday, a lace hankie and daubed at the tear.

"But he wasn't a stranger," she remembered saying. "Not exactly. Clarence Dibble introduced us."

"What's the man's name?" J.W. had said.

"His name is Richard Fuller."

"He's a gambler, isn't he?" Mollie said.

"Well, yes, but —."

J.W. had interrupted her.

"Baby, we just want to protect you. That's all. A man like that — he's no good. He'll just wind up hurting you, and we don't want you hurt. Can't you see that?"

"I suppose you'd rather have me dance all night with Dalton Bradley," Ellie said. "I suppose you think he's decent. He tried to get me outside tonight, but I wouldn't go. All Richard did was dance and talk with me. He never tried anything else."

"We don't think you should have spent the entire evening dancing with any one young man," Mollie said. "A young lady should dance with several different young men. The thing that bothered us about this evening was the fact that you spent it all with this gambler."

"With Richard," Ellie said.

"Whatever his name is," Mollie said.

"Anyway, I don't see why I should spend time with boys who are boring and stuck up when I can spend it with a man who is interesting to be with," Ellie said.

Then J.W. decided to bring the whole discussion to a close.

"All right," he said. "It's all over and done now. You won't be seeing him again anyway, so let's all stop fussing with each other. You know how we feel. No more need be said. Good night."

And there was no more said that night. But two nights later, Richard Fuller came riding out to the ranch. J.W. met him out on the porch.

"Don't bother climbing down out of the saddle, young man," J.W. said. "I got nothing against you personally, but I don't want you seeing my daughter."

"Excuse me, sir," Fuller said, "but I don't believe we've even met. May I ask what your objections to me might be?"

"I object to your profession, mister. You are a gambler, aren't you?"

"Yes, sir, I am, but I'm an honest gambler. I've never cheated anyone, and I never will, and I make a decent living. And it's legal. Have you never played a game of cards?"

"Sure, I've played, but I don't make my living at it."

"Is the cattle business any less a gamble than what I do?" Fuller said. "You gamble that the price of beef will go up or at least stay where it is. But it might go down. You gamble on the weather. You—."

"I don't intend to stand here and argue with you," J.W. said. "I'm asking you to get off of my property."

11

Fuller touched the brim of his hat and nodded toward J.W. as he started backing his horse away from the porch.

"I don't have to be told twice, Mr. McKee," he said. "I didn't come here intending to start any trouble. Good evening to you, sir."

But just then Ellie came out the front door. She looked at Fuller, then at her father.

"Richard," she said. "What happened?"

"I'm afraid I've been ordered off the property by your father," he said. "I'm sorry. I just wanted to talk to you."

"Father," Ellie said, starting to protest, but J.W. did not allow her to finish.

"Get back in the house, Ellie," he said. Ellie turned and ran back into the house. She was confused and frustrated with this new element in her life. Never before had her parents refused her anything. Never before had they issued orders. She did not understand it, and she did not like it. Furthermore, she did not intend to allow it to continue. She ran back into the house, but she went straight through and out the back door. She ran out to the corral where she ordered the first cowhand she saw to saddle her horse for her. Then she mounted up and raced after Fuller. It didn't take her long to catch him, and she then led the way off the path to a secluded spot where they could talk without fear of interruption. She apologized for her father's rude behavior, and she told him that she was glad he had come to see her. The conversation was brief, Fuller insisting that he did not want her to have any trouble with her parents on his account. It had been brief, but it ended with a kiss and a promise to meet again.

For the next four weeks there were secret meetings. As far as Ellie knew, J.W. and Mollie were blissfully ignorant of what was happening around them. Ellie did not say another word to them about Fuller, and they seemed to have forgotten all about the one unpleasant evening they had experienced with their daughter. The meetings often took the form of long rides in the country. Occasionally Ellie managed to pack a picnic basket. They talked and laughed together, and finally the inevitable happened. They made love. It happened under the open sky in broad daylight, and Ellie whispered into Fuller's ear, "I love you, Richard," and she meant it with all her heart. She just naturally assumed, after what they had done together, what they had done to each other, for each other, that he, too, loved her. He had not, however, said so, and she was aware of that little omission. She thought that he was just shy, perhaps, and that he would say it later. But there was not a later. She did not see him again after that day. She became moody, thoughtful and sad, and her long rides the afternoons ceased. J.W. and Mollie noticed the change in her behavior and in her disposition, and they were worried about her. They tried to get her to talk to them about it, but to no avail. Her answers were always evasive.

Six weeks passed by the time she received the letter. It had been mailed from a town in Texas called Jubilation.

Dear Ellie,

I know you must think me a heel for running out on you the way I did, and I call myself worse names ten times a day. I did not mean to take advantage of you, and I never meant to hurt you. What happened between us just happened. It was wonderful. It was beautiful, and I was on the verge of expressing to you the fact

13

that I was falling in love with you, but I had to bite my tongue. I am a roving gambler, and you could never have a life with me. I am just not cut out for marriage, and so I decided that it would be better for you if I just slipped away out of your life for good. I did that, but I've been tormented by my decision ever since, so I had to write to you and try to explain. If you can find it in your heart to forgive me, please do so. If not, I understand, but please believe me when I say that in my own peculiar way, I love you, and if I have hurt you in any way, I am truly sorry.

Richard Fuller

About that same time, Ellie began to suspect the worst, and she knew that what had happened to her was exactly what her parents had worried about. She was pregnant, and the man who was the father of the child had fled.

Chapter Two

Coker Jack had a broad grin across his face. He had good reason for it. He was winning big. Directly across the table, Richard Fuller stared hard as Coker Jack raked in his winnings from the last hand. The deck was passed to Coker Jack. It was his deal. Besides Coker Jack and Fuller, there were three men at the table: Donald Kane, the son of Sheriff Ben Kane, Deputy Sheriff Denver Bond and a man known only as Conley. Coker Jack had been the big winner, but the heaviest losses had been Fuller's. Still staring at Coker Jack, Fuller reached inside his coat and withdrew his wallet. He still had some cash on the table in front of him. He picked it up, tucked it into the wallet and replaced the wallet in his inside coat pocket. Coker Jack glanced up in time to see what Fuller had done.

"You're not quitting, are you?" he said.

"I've had enough," said Fuller. He pushed back his chair and stood up.

"You can't win back your money if you quit,"

said Coker Jack.

"I guess not," said Fuller, "but then, I don't think there's much chance of me winning anything in this game anyhow."

Conley stood up from his chair.

"I think he's right," he said. "I'm out."

Conley turned and walked away. Coker Jack hardly looked at him. He was staring back at Fuller. Slowly Coker Jack pushed his chair away from the table, and slowly he stood up facing Fuller. He pushed his long coattails back to reveal two six-shooters, one hanging on each hip.

"What's wrong, Fuller?" he said.

Fuller didn't answer, but he stood his ground.

"What'd you mean by that remark you made?" said Coker Jack.

"I meant what I said," said Fuller. "No more, no less. Forget it."

"No," said Coker Jack. "No. You don't drop a line like that and then just walk away. I think you meant to say that I been cheating."

"Mister," said Fuller, "if I'd meant to say that, there wouldn't be any question. I'd have said it straight out."

He turned his back on Coker Jack and started to walk toward the door.

"Fuller," said Coker Jack, "you can talk plainer than that."

Fuller stopped. He stood still for a moment, then slowly turned to face Coker Jack once again. He heaved a sigh of exasperation.

"You're just determined to make me call you a cheat, aren't you?" he said. "All right. I'll say it as plain as I know how. I think you're a cheat. I can't prove it, or I wouldn't be walking away from here, but I'm satisfied in my own mind, and I won't play cards with you."

Coker Jack's hands went for his guns, but before he had a chance to pull either one from its holster, a tiny Remington .41 caliber Double Derringer appeared in Fuller's right hand. It was cocked and aimed at Coker Jack's chest. Coker Jack slowly moved his hands out away from his sides, away from the gun butts. He smiled.

"I still say let's forget the whole thing," said Fuller. "What do you say?"

Coker Jack laughed, a short snort of a laugh.

"Sure," he said. "That's what I say. Let's just forget the whole damn thing. No harm done."

Fuller eased the hammer down on his Derringer, turned his back once more on Coker Jack and walked out of the saloon. Deputy Sheriff Denver Bond scooted his chair backward to reveal the fact that he had been holding a cocked revolver in his lap under the table pointed toward Coker Jack. The surprise display was not lost on Coker Jack. He shot a glance at the gun, but he quickly regained his composure and laughed again. He sat back down.

"Well," he said, "let's play cards."

Bond stood up and holstered his gun.

"Not me," he said, and he turned to walk away.

Donald Kane, too, stood up as if to leave.

"Sit down, College boy," said Coker Jack. "Everyone else has run out on me. You've got to stay."

Donald glared at Coker Jack.

"You've got most of my money already," he said.

Coker Jack chuckled and shuffled the deck of cards.

"Most ain't good enough, Donnie," he said. "Come on. Let's play cards."

Denver Bond had walked over to the bar where he had ordered himself a shot of whiskey. He was standing beside a brazenly painted young woman who gave the appearance of having crammed a whole lot of living into a few short years.

"How are you, Lottie?" said Bond.

"I'm scared, Denver," she said. "All the girls are."

"If you'd just say yes to me, you'd be out of it," said Bond.

"Oh, Denver," she said, a whine in her voice.

"All right," he said. "This ain't the place to talk about it anyhow. I'll see you after awhile. Okay?"

"Sure, Denver. You know it's okay. I'll be waiting for you."

He tossed down the rest of his drink and went outside. Richard Fuller was standing on the board sidewalk, leaning against a post. Bond walked over to stand beside him.

"You handled that situation in there pretty well, Fuller," he said.

"He's a cheap tinhorn," said Fuller. "Anybody could handle him. Besides, I saw your gun under the table."

"You saw that?" said Bond. "I didn't think anybody saw it."

"Well, I did."

Bond shook his head.

"Say, Fuller," he said. "Was he really cheating?"

"Like I said before," said Fuller, "I couldn't prove it."

"Just between you and me," said Bond. "We ain't in no courtroom."

Fuller looked into Bond's face for a long moment. Then he looked away again, staring out into the street.

"He was cheating," he said.

"The son of a bitch," said Bond.

"It's a damn shame when a man can't find an honest card game," said Fuller.

"Yeah," said Bond. "Damn shame. You know, I was all prepared to just write it off to nerves. You know. Everyone's jumpy around this town these days, what with those killings we've had."

"No clues yet?" asked Fuller.

"Not a damn thing," said the deputy. "Nothing."

"What kind of a man would go around killing girls with a knife?" said Fuller. "I hope you catch him soon. That's one hanging I'd like to witness."

"Not girls," said Bond. "Whores."

"What difference does that make?"

"It makes a big difference to some men. Big difference."

Sheriff Ben Kane came walking down the sidewalk toward where Fuller and Bond stood talking. Bond looked up at the approaching sheriff.

"Howdy, Ben," he said. Then he slapped Fuller on the shoulder. "You take it easy," he said. "That was a good job you did in there."

As the sheriff came alongside him, Bond turned and fell in step with him. They walked a little ways on down the sidewalk before Kane spoke.

"What was that you were talking about to that gambler?" he said.

"Oh," said Bond, "Fuller caught Coker Jack cheating in there a little while ago. Well, he didn't actually catch him at it. He was just suspicious. He quit the game, and Coker Jack, he started pressing Fuller to tell him why he was quitting. Fuller finally told him, and Coker Jack went for his guns. Old Fuller come up with a pea-shooter. I think it's a sleeve gun. Anyhow, he covered Coker Jack and backed him down without a shot fired."

"Hunh," said Kane. "Gambling always leads to trouble."

Bond pretended not to have heard that comment. He had gotten used to ignoring the sheriff's pious platitudes.

"Was—was Donald in the game?" said Kane.

"Yes, sir," said Bond. "I'm afraid he was. Still is, matter of fact."

Kane scowled but said nothing more. The two men walked on down the street and turned in at the door to the sheriff's office.

Coker Jack's pockets were full of other people's money, and his belly was full of good whiskey. It had been a long day, and he had spent most of it in the Rattlesnake Saloon. Toward the end of the day, he had stopped playing cards long enough to order a good meal. Then he had played some more and drunk some more whiskey. Finally he had decided to call it a day, a good day, a profitable day. He was happy. There had been one minor incident. Richard Fuller had practically accused him of cheating, and he had done so right in front of the others. But what did Coker Jack care about that? Fuller couldn't prove anything. He had said so out loud. And Coker Jack had a good deal of Fuller's money mixed in with the rest.

So to hell with Fuller. To hell with him and all the rest. It was dark outside when Coker Jack left the Rattlesnake. Even the few new-fangled electric lights along Jubilation's main street were turned out for the night. He stopped for a moment out on the board sidewalk and breathed in the cool night air. Then he reached into his inside coat pocket for a cigar. He bit off the end and spat it out. Then he fumbled in his pockets for a match. Finally locating one, he struck it on the pole there and lit the cigar.

Life, he thought, was just too, too good. After a couple of puffs on the cigar, he turned and started walking toward the hotel. His walk was unsteady. He was just a little surprised to find himself quite that drunk. But what did it matter? He walked on, weaving his way down the sidewalk. Once he bumped against one of the posts which held up the overhanging roof of a storefront. He overcompensated and staggered into the wall on the other side of the walk. He stopped, pulled himself up straight, took a couple of deep breaths and resumed his walk, taking care to walk in a straight line. That resolve lasted only four steps. He found himself wobbling again. He lurched over to the inside edge of the walk and leaned against a storefront.

"Hah," he said out loud. "Whew. I had more of that stuff than I thought. Just a little drunk here. Just a little. I'll just stagger my way on to the hotel and up the stairs and then I'll be just fine. Just fine. Old Coker Jack is just fine."

He took a few more deep breaths and started walking again. He came to the end of the sidewalk, the end of the row of buildings which were attached to each other, and he almost fell as he stepped off the walk and down onto the ground. The next building was the hotel, but there was a space between it and the last building Coker Jack had passed. It was a long, narrow space leading back to the alley, and it was pitch black in there. As Coker Jack staggered by, a shadowy figure stepped out of the black passageway behind him and swung a club. It struck Coker Jack a glancing blow to the back of the head.

He screamed and turned instinctively to face his attacker. A second blow caught him in the center of his forehead. It landed with a solid thunk, and Coker Jack's knees buckled, and he took two faltering backward steps, but he managed to stay on his feet. His hands went up defensively to his face and head, and he could feel the hot, sticky blood running down his face, into his eyes and between his fingers. The shadowy figure swung again, and the club broke fingers as it landed on its target. Coker Jack screamed again. And the club was drawn back, and again it was swung, this time with more force than before. Knuckles were crunched against skull. Coker Jack was by this time blind with pain and fear and rage. It was dark, and he was drunk, and now he was battered, and his eyes were filled with blood. He roared out in a combination of anger and terror. He howled like some dying beast, and he sank to his knees. The club descended again, and there was a ghastly cracking sound, followed by a weak and low groan from Coker Jack. Again the club came down, and again it cracked skull. Coker Jack pitched forward in the dirt. The mysterious figure swung the club again and again, and the last time the club struck the head of the limp thing there in the dark that had so recently been the happily drunken Coker Jack, it landed with a sickening squishy sound.

The figure stepped back into the deep darkness of the narrow passageway and waited. There was no one in the street. No lights came on. No one was running toward the scene. Apparently no one had seen or heard anything. Or if they had, they were too cowed by the recent murders to venture out into the night. The figure stepped out again and knelt beside the body. It felt the pockets of Coker Jack's coat, and it found great rolls of bills which it then stuffed into its own pockets. It very carefully went through all the pockets of the clothing on the body.

Then it stood up, looked around once more, and vanished into the dark corridor which ran between the two buildings.

Denver Bond stepped out on the upstairs landing of a room on the backside of the Rattlesnake Saloon. He pulled his hat down tight on his head. Lottie Kuntz was standing in the doorway. She was barely dressed.

"I'd stay with you, Lottie," he said, "but I've got to make my rounds. It's part of my job."

"I know, Denver," she said. "Don't worry about me. I'll be all right."

"Lock this door," said Bond. "And keep that other one locked. Don't let anyone in."

"I might have to let someone in, Denver," she said. "It's part of my job."

"Damn it," said Bond. "I wish you wouldn't talk like that. Why don't you let me take you away from all this? We could—."

"Don't," she said. "We've been all through that before. Go on now. I'll be all right."

"Just be careful," he said.

Lottie kissed him on the lips.

"Good night," she said, and she shut the door. He stood there on the landing and listened for the sound of the latch. Then he walked down the stairs. He tried to take his mind off of Lottie and his worries concerning her. Walking the streets at night, he was a lawman on duty, and he had to be alert. There had been three recent murders in Jubilation. He couldn't afford to walk around with his mind abstracted. He checked the door on the back of the saloon on the ground level and found it locked. Then he walked around to the front of the building and checked the door there. It too was locked. He began making his way methodically down the street, checking each store front as he passed it by. He knew this routine by heart. If anything was out of place anywhere, he would know it in an instant. He was proud of his knowledge of the town. He was moving in the direction of the Imperial Hotel. It was a dark night, and there were few lights on the main street of the town. The sky was clear though, and the air was not really cold, but cool and crisp. He stepped down off the end of the board sidewalk, took two more steps and stumbled.

"What—? Damn," he said.

Then he saw the body.

Chapter Three

When the train pulled into the station, Ellie was up and to the end of the aisle in a minute. She only had one small bag, aside from her purse. She had left home in a hurry, in secret and on horseback. She had to travel light. She stepped out on the platform there at the station, and looked in both directions. It was a bustling little town. Over the heads of the people crowding the streets, she could see the sign for a hotel and another for a saloon. There was a general store and a blacksmith's shop. She did not see what she was looking for. She went inside the depot and walked up to the counter. A man was there ahead of her paying for a ticket. When he was done, she stepped up to the counter. The clerk was looking terribly busy with ticket stubs, receipts, ledger books and various other scraps of paper.

"Excuse me," she said.

The clerk looked up with an annoyed expression on his face.

"Where is the stage station?" she said.

"You're in the railroad depot, ma'am," said the clerk.

"I know where I am," she said. "Please tell me where the stage station is."

"Where do you want to go?" he said.

"I want to go to the stage station."

"Down the street," he said. "West. South side of the street."

"Thank you," she said in as icy a voice as she could manage. She turned and walked briskly out of the depot and headed west down the street. Two or three different men smiled and tipped their hats as she passed them by, and one bold fellow asked if he could help her with her bag.

"No, thank you," she said without slowing her pace and without looking at the man. The station was clear at the far end of the street. When she got there, she went inside.

"I need to get to Jubilation as soon as possible," she said. "When do you have a stagecoach going that way?"

"The stage should be pulling in here in about an hour," said the man. "Be about a half hour or so after that before it turns around to head back south."

"I'd like a ticket, please."

She paid the man and got her ticket.

"May I leave my bag here?"

"Sure. I'll take it and put it right back here behind the counter."

"Thank you," she said. She handed him the bag.

"It'll be right here when you're ready to leave."

"How long will the trip take?" she asked.

"You'll stop overnight in a place called Dog Track. It's not really a town. Just a stopover. A station. But it has private accommodations for ladies. You'll get into Jubilation tomorrow evening. I'd say around seven."

"Thank you very much," said Ellie. "I'll be back in time for the stage. Is there a post office in town?"

"Just a little ways down the street and on the other side."

Ellie posted a letter and then found a small cafe where she sat down to have coffee and a roll. She had money, but she didn't know how long it would have to last her. What if Richard had left Jubilation by the time she got there? She tried not to think of that possibility too much, but she knew that she was taking a chance. He was, after all, a gambler, and like most gamblers, a drifter. Well, she would change all that. Still, she had to watch her money. She'd had a little left from the last time she'd gone shopping. She had never before worried about money. If she wanted something, she simply asked her father, and he would give her the money she needed. But this time she couldn't ask him. She had not even told him she was leaving. She couldn't tell him what she had done, what had happened to her. Not until she had taken care of the situation in the proper manner. When she had her husband, she would take him home to the ranch.

Sipping her coffee, she wondered how J.W. and Mollie would react when her letter arrived. "Don't worry," she had written. "I'm all right, and I know what I'm doing. Sampson has not been stolen. I rode him into town, and then I sold him to Mr. Talley as I needed some money for my trip. When I return it will be with a husband. You see, I'm going to have Richard's baby. He doesn't know yet, so I'm going to find him and tell him, and then we will be married. If you'll have us after that, and if Richard agrees, we'll stay at the ranch. But if I've hurt you too badly, then we'll leave. I love you both very much, and I'm terribly sorry to have caused you this concern. But once again, please don't worry. I'll take care of everything. Everything will turn out just fine."

And she believed with all her heart that it would. She would find Richard, and he would marry her. He would also settle down. She would see to that. Her child was not going to grow up with a gambler for a father. She had not liked sneaking away from her parents like a thief, and she had not liked having to sell Sampson, the big, beautiful, red stallion that J.W. had given her on her seventeenth birthday. But those things had to be done. She had gotten herself into this fix, against the strong advice and protests of her parents, and she would get herself out of it.

When the waitress offered her a refill of coffee, she checked the time, and finding that she had plenty of leeway, accepted. Tomorrow night, she mused, she would be in Jubilation. She had left the ranch on Sampson, sold Sampson in town and purchased a railroad ticket. She had ridden the train as far south into Texas as it would take her, and soon she would board the stagecoach to go on into Jubilation, a rough ride of a day and a half. There she would find Richard, and everything would be all right. She knew that it would.

She paid for her roll and coffee and walked back down the street to the stage station. The stagecoach was there, and it was facing south. Apparently it had arrived while she was in the cafe, and it had already been prepared for its return trip. The horses looked fresh. Ellie hurried inside for her bag. Going through the door, she almost ran into a big man in a suit that seemed just a bit too small for him.

"Excuse me, Miss," said the man.

"It's quite all right," said Ellie. "Actually I think it was my fault."

She got her bag from the clerk and went back outside. Soon her bag was stowed in the boot, and she was seated inside the coach facing forward. The big man in the small suit struggled into the coach and took a seat facing Ellie. He smiled a bit awkwardly.

"Hello again," he said.

"Hello," said Ellie.

"It looks like we're going to be traveling together."

"It looks like," she said.

"Are you going all the way to Jubilation?" he asked.

"Yes, I am."

"My name is Franklin Smith," he said.

"I'm Ellie McKee."

Smith offered his hand, and Ellie took it, but Smith held on to her hand a little too long for comfort. She pulled it loose.

"Oh," said Smith. "Sorry."

His ears turned slightly red.

"It's all right," said Ellie.

A man and woman climbed into the coach. The

man sat beside Smith, the woman beside Ellie.

"Did our bags get loaded?" said the woman.

"Yes, dear," said the man. "I watched them."

"Good," said the woman.

She looked at Ellie.

"How do you do," she said. "I'm Charlotte Higgins."

"Ellie McKee," said Ellie. "I'm pleased to meet you."

"This is my husband, Nelson."

"How do you do, Mr. Higgins," said Ellie. "This gentleman is Mr. — ?"

"Franklin Smith," said Smith. "Glad to meet you folks."

"Well," said Mrs. Higgins, "it will be a godsend when this part of Texas catches up to the rest of the world. Stagecoach travel in this day and age. It's absurd. We only just got electricity in our house."

"Really?" said Ellie.

"Yes, indeed," said Mrs. Higgins. "We're trying to get telephone lines in, but the company's being difficult."

From up above the driver's voice bellowed out.

"Hang onto your hats, folks," he shouted. "We're on the way."

They heard the sound of the brake being released, the snap of a whip and a shout, and the stage moved forward with a sudden lurch. They were, indeed, on the way. Ellie felt a deep sense of relief. There were no more changes to be made, no more tickets to be bought. With the exception of the overnight stopover at Dog Track, the next stop would be Jubilation, the end of her journey.

But the ride in the stagecoach was even rougher

than Ellie had anticipated. They jounced, jerked, bounced and rolled from side to side. Now and then one or the other or all of them would nearly be thrown from their seats. But soon Ellie became almost grateful for the rough ride, for when the going was at its smoothest, the small talk of Mr. and Mrs. Higgins was a dreadful bore, and the attempts at friendly conversation by Smith were even worse. The man reached over and patted her hand once or twice, and once he even missed, probably on purpose, and patted her on the leg. He was beginning to be a nuisance, and she decided that sooner or later she would have to put him in his place.

It seemed to Ellie like an incredibly long day and a nearly endless distance to Dog Track, but they finally arrived, and Ellie felt as if she had just been released from a tiny cell. Her whole body felt cramped, and her brain as well felt like it had been pressed upon by her fellow passengers in the cramped coach. She spent several minutes just walking around and breathing in the fresh air. Then Smith was there beside her.

"Are you all right?" he said.

"Of course, I'm all right," said Ellie. "why wouldn't I be?"

"Well," he said, "it was a rough ride. I just wanted to make sure you were all right."

"Mr. Smith," she said, trying hard to let her voice express her annoyance with his attention to her, "please don't bother yourself over my well being. I'm perfectly capable of taking care of myself."

"This is rough country for a lady all alone," said Smith. "A lady should have a man to look after her."

"I'm meeting my fiance in Jubilation," said Ellie, "and we're going to be married. In the meantime, I can manage quite well."

Smith's ears turned red, and he ducked his head to look at the ground.

"I see," he said. "Well, if there's anything I can do, let me know. Excuse me."

Just then the driver stepped out of the station house. He put a hand to the side of his mouth and gave a yell.

"Come and get it," he said. "Soup's on."

Ellie made a beeline for the station house with Smith trailing along dejectedly behind her. The meal was not great, but it would do. It was mostly potatoes and beans with a little salt pork for flavoring and a platter of hard biscuits. The best thing about it, Ellie thought, was that the price was included in the stage fare. She ate heartily and drank several cups of coffee. The agent for the stage line who had sold her the ticket had not lied about Dog Track. There wasn't much to it: the station house, a stable with a corral in front and a makeshift saloon in a canvas tent with a sign out front that read, "Watering Hole." The accommodations for the passengers for the overnight stay were basic. One end of the big room in the station house was partitioned off by a canvas curtain. Behind the canvas were cots for the men. There was a small room in the back with cots for the women. Back there privacy was provided for each lady by a canvas divider between the beds. The ladies retired early, as did Mr. Higgins, at the insistence of his wife, but the stagecoach driver and his shotgun rider along with Franklin Smith adjourned to the Watering Hole.

The cot was not comfortable, and the insurances of privacy were not convincing, but Ellie soon dropped off to sleep in spite of all that. It had been a long and hard day. She worked her way in dreams through fitful images of lurching coaches and speeding trains, and she had settled down to a peaceful vision of a happy meeting with Richard. As she approached him, he smiled and held out his arms to welcome her in a loving embrace. Then she was awakened by a sudden loud shriek very near. She sat up straight in her cot, reached down to the floor for her handbag, opened it and stuck her hand inside. There was the sound of a slap and then another and then the sound of a body falling over something. And there were voices. She thought that she recognized the voice of Mrs. Higgins.

"Animal," it said. "Brute. What do you think you're doing? Get out. Get out. Nelson. Nelson. Where are you?"

Then came the other voice.

"Wait," it said. "Please. It's all a mistake. I'm sorry. I didn't realize. I thought you were—."

"Animal," shouted Mrs. Higgins.

The door to the big room opened, and the driver stepped in with a lantern in one hand and a Colt .45 in the other.

"What the hell's going on in here?" he said.

Ellie stood up and pulled back the canvas curtain that separated her compartment from that of Mrs. Higgins, who was standing up beside her cot, a sheet held up before her, although she was well covered by her nightgown. On the far side of the cot, trying to scramble back up to his feet was Franklin Smith. His whole head was red.

33

"It's all a stupid mistake," he said. "I—I must have had too much to drink. I just wandered into the wrong room."

"That's not what it sounded like to me," said Ellie.

"What?" said Smith. For the first time he saw Ellie standing there beside the canvas curtain.

"I heard you start to say something a moment ago," said Ellie. "You said that you thought she was—. What? What did you think, Mr. Smith? Whose bed did you think you were getting into?"

Smith stood up on shaky legs. He looked at Mrs. Higgins with the ferocious, unforgiving expression on her face, and he looked at the driver whose Colt was aimed generally in Smith's direction. Then he looked back at Ellie.

"No," he said. "No. You misunderstood. I just meant to go to bed. In my bed. That's all."

"I hope so, Mr. Smith," said Ellie. "But just in case you're lying, in case you thought that you were getting into my bed, I want you to know that your mistake was a lucky one. I wouldn't have screamed. I would have killed you."

She brought her right hand out from behind the canvas to reveal her .38 caliber Webley British Bulldog revolver.

"All right," said the driver, deciding to take control of the situation, "are you going to accept his story, Miss?"

"Sure," said Ellie, lowering the Webley. "It was all a mistake."

"How about you, Ma'am?"

"Oh, all right," said Mrs. Higgins. "Just get him out of here, please."

Mr. Higgins appeared in the doorway behind the

34

driver and peeked around the other man to see into the room.

"What's happening?" he said.

"Everyone just go on back to bed," said the driver. "But get into the right beds."

Chapter Four

What had been Coker Jack was laid out and covered over in Vance Muldrow's Undertaking Parlor, and Ben Kane and Denver Bond were back at the scene of the crime once again. There were footprints, but they had been obscured to the point where they were no help at all. They had already discovered the club, a short ax handle, one end matted with blood and bits of hair. It had been put away in the sheriff's office. The body had been searched, and it had been determined that Coker Jack had been robbed after the bludgeoning. There was no money in the pockets.

"The wages of sin," said Kane. "You said that Coker Jack had been playing poker yesterday, didn't you?"

"That's right," said Bond.

"Cheating maybe?"

"Probably," corrected Bond.

"Did he win?"

"He was the big winner, all right," said Bond. "He should have had a bundle on him."

"Come on," said Kane. "Let's check his hotel room before we jump to any conclusions."

They were just beside the hotel anyway. Kane led the way on over to the front door, and they went inside.

"Tony," said Kane, his voice demanding.

Tony Arnall looked up from his place behind the counter.

"Oh, hello, Sheriff," he said. "Hi, Denver. What can I do for y'all?"

"Tony," said Kane, "when did you see Coker Jack yesterday?"

"He left out of here about ten in the morning, Ben," said Arnall, "and I never seen him again. It's awful what happened to him. And just outside too. You got to catch whoever it is doing these killings, Ben. None of us is safe here."

"What do you think we're doing here, Tony?" said Kane. "Could he have come back to his room anytime during the day or night before he was killed and you not know it?"

"It's possible, I guess," said Arnall, "but it ain't likely. See, I didn't get no relief yesterday. Ernie's home sick to his stomach. I even had to have my meals brought in, and I ate right here at the counter. I suppose he could have sneaked in and got past me, but why would he want to do that?"

"Let me have the key to his room," said Kane.

Arnall found a key and handed it to the sheriff. Kane went upstairs followed closely by Bond. They found Coker Jack's room and unlocked it. Once inside, they searched the room thoroughly. They found nothing of any particular interest, nothing to help with the investigation. They found no money. Kane sat down on the edge of the bed. Bond thought that Kane had aged considerably in a very short time. The rash of murders that Jubilation was experiencing had taken their toll on the old man. The killing of Coker Jack was the fourth in less than that many months.

"So what do we know?" said Kane.

"What?" said Bond. He had been lost in his own thoughts.

"What do we know about this?"

"Well," said Bond, "somebody beat Coker Jack's brains in last night. Probably late. He used that old ax handle."

"And?"

"And he robbed him. I know that Coker Jack had a bundle of cash yesterday. There was no money on the body, and there ain't none in his room here."

"That's what it looks like," said Kane. "Of course, he could have put his money in the bank. I doubt it, but it's possible. Check it out, will you? Then meet me over at the Rattlesnake."

"Sure thing, Ben," said Bond, and he left the room. Ben Kane sat there on the edge of the bed and stared at the floor. He was tired. He was so damned tired, but he had to keep going. This thing had to be taken care of. He leaned forward, put his hands on his knees and shoved, heaving himself to his feet with a loud groan. He looked around the room one more time, then went downstairs. Passing by the counter, he tossed the key back to Tony Arnall.

"Thanks, Tony," he said, and he kept walking toward the door.

"You find anything up there, Sheriff?" said Arnall.

Kane didn't bother answering the question. He pushed the door open and walked out onto the sidewalk. Looking down the street, he could see Denver Bond just going into the bank. He drew in a raspy breath and started walking toward the Rattlesnake.

Inside the Rattlesnake, Richard Fuller sat at a table alone. In front of him on the table were a bottle of whiskey and a glass. In his hands was a deck of cards. Ben Kane walked in and went straight to the bar where he got a cup of coffee from the bartender. Then he turned to lean sideways against the bar so that he could watch Fuller. He was still in that posture sipping his coffee when Denver Bond came in and walked over to join him.

"Want a cup of coffee, Denver?" said Kane.

"No," said Bond. "I've done had too much coffee for one day. What are we doing here, Ben?"

"Let's go over there and have a talk with that gambler."

"Fuller?"

"Yeah. That one."

"What for?"

"Come on," said Kane. He carried his coffee with him as he walked over to the table where Fuller sat shuffling cards. Bond followed, a little hesitant.

"Mind if we sit down?" said Kane.

Fuller looked up.

"Not at all, Sheriff," he said. "You play cards?"

"I don't believe in card playing," said Kane. "It's a sin in the eyes of the Lord."

"It's legal," said Fuller.

"That don't make it right."

Bond stood a couple of paces behind Sheriff Kane, looking uneasy, a little embarrassed even. Kane pulled out a chair and sat down. He crossed his arms over his chest and stared at Fuller. Bond also took a chair.

"Well," said Fuller, "if it's not a card game you're looking for, then it must be something else. What's on your mind?"

"You were playing cards in here yesterday," said Kane.

"Sure I was," said Fuller. "That's the way I make my living. I try to play every day. I haven't been able to scare up a game today. Otherwise I'd be playing right now."

"I'm talking about yesterday," said Kane. "You played with Coker Jack, didn't you?"

"With Coker Jack, with a man named Conley, and with your deputy there," said Fuller. "Oh, yeah. And with your boy, Donald. Yeah. So what?"

"Who won?" said the sheriff.

"Coker Jack was the big winner," said Fuller. He shot a glance at Bond. "But I think you know all that already."

"Who was the big loser?" said the sheriff.

Fuller shuffled his deck of cards. He looked up at Kane.

"That depends on how you look at it," he said.

"I lost more than anybody else, but I still had money in my pocket when I left the game. How about you, Mr. Bond?"

"He busted me," said Bond.

"I'm asking you, Fuller," said Kane, and his voice was more firm, almost angry. His expression had grown more tense.

"All I'm saying, Sheriff," said Fuller, "is that a man who loses his last ten dollars is a bigger loser than a man who loses a thousand but still has another thousand in his pocket. Yeah. I lost more money than anyone else in the game. Is that what you want to know?"

"And you had a fight with Coker Jack right after the game," said Kane.

"I wouldn't call it that," said Fuller. "I quit playing, and he didn't want me to. He kept pestering me until I finally told him that I suspected him of cheating. Then he went for his guns. I got the drop on him first. That's all."

"Is it?"

"Yeah. It is."

"You expect me to believe that a professional gambler would just walk away from a game when he'd been cheated?" said Kane.

"I knew that I was being cheated," said Fuller, "but I couldn't prove it, so I walked away. Yeah. Believe what you want."

Bond leaned forward on the table nervously. He tentatively raised a hand in an attempt to get attention.

"Ben," he said. "Ben, I think that Fuller here handled that situation real well. He tried to just walk away from that game. Coker Jack pushed him. Even then he didn't come right out and call Coker Jack a cheat, and then Coker Jack went for his guns first, just like Fuller said."

The sheriff tipped up his cup and drank the last of his coffee. He put the cup down on the table and stood up.

"Last night," he said, "someone in this town took an axe handle and caved in Coker Jack's skull. Then he cleaned out his pockets. Earlier the same day a man lost a whole bunch of money to Coker Jack and then pulled a gun on him. Called him a cheat. That just naturally makes me want to ask questions. By the way, Fuller, where were you when Coker Jack's brains was being bashed?"

"Well, I suppose I was in my room," said Fuller. "I went there right after I saw you two out on the street."

"No alibi," said Kane.

"Wait a minute," said Fuller, rising to his feet. "What do I need with an alibi? You've had a series of murders in this town. Is it four? Four now? The other three took place before I even came to town."

"Those other three killings don't have anything to do with this one," said Kane.

"How can you be so sure?" said Fuller.

Bond gave Kane a questioning look, as if he, too, would like to hear the answer to that question.

"The first three killings were done by some kind of crazy man. Like that Englishman. What'd they call him? The Ripper. Jack the Ripper. He killed whores with a knife. That's all. No robbery. No nothing. He just killed whores."

Bond gritted his teeth and looked away. Kane continued.

42

"This was a mad killing and a robbery. A man don't bash a man's head in like that unless he's damn mad at him. After he was done, he robbed him. No, sir. There's no connection between them whore killings and this one. None whatsoever."

Kane turned and walked out of the saloon. Fuller looked at Bond, and Bond gave a shrug.

"Hell, Fuller," he said, "I guess if I hadn't been here, maybe I'd be asking you the same questions. I don't know. I guess he's got to ask them."

"I guess," said Fuller.

"Hey, Fuller?"

"Yeah?"

"You ever heard about that Englishman? The one Ben named. I can't recall what he called him."

"Jack the Ripper," said Fuller. "Yeah. It was back in 'eighty-eight, I think. Somebody in London, England, knifed a bunch of women. I think they were all prostitutes. I'm not sure. Anyhow, they never caught him. Never even figured out who he was."

"Ben thinks he done it?"

"Someone like him," said Fuller.

"We ain't got no Englishmen in town. Have we?"

"Not that I've run into. But he wouldn't have to be English," said Fuller. "Just someone like Jack the Ripper, someone who wants to kill—ladies of the night—with a knife."

"That's crazy," said Bond.

"That's just what the sheriff said," said Fuller. "Now you're catching on. But your sheriff thinks that I killed Coker Jack."

"Aw," said Bond, "you didn't do it. Did you?"

"No, I didn't. If I'd wanted to kill the man, I'd

have done it right in here yesterday afternoon, with you watching."

"That's what I thought. Anyhow, if Ben's right, we got two killers in town."

"Yeah," said Fuller, standing up from his chair. "And I'm glad that it's your problem and not mine. See you later. I'm going to the hotel."

"Yeah," said Bond. "See you."

Bond stood and watched Fuller leave the Rattlesnake. Then he walked over to the bar. He leaned across to speak to the bartender confidentially.

"Arch," he said, "where's Lottie?"

"She's upstairs with a customer, Denver."

"Oh," said Bond. "Okay. Thanks."

Bond turned and walked away. He went out the front door of the Rattlesnake, then down the sidewalk, around the corner and back to the alley. He walked to a back stairway and climbed it to a landing. A door there let him in on the second floor. He closed the door behind himself and leaned against the wall, staring down the hallway toward another closed door, and he waited.

Richard Fuller went to his room in the hotel and pulled his carpetbag out from under the bed. He opened the drawers to the bureau and began tossing his clothing into the bag. Kane was trying to pin the murder of Coker Jack on him, and he didn't intend to stay around Jubilation to be railroaded into jail—or worse. The mood people were in around these parts, he thought, any twelve men would send anyone else to the gallows just to see someone hang. There had been four mysterious

44

deaths, and there were two murderers loose in the streets. Two? Yes. He admitted that he had to agree with Kane on that. The man who bashed Coker Jack's brains out was not likely to be the same man who knifed three prostitutes. But people wanted to see a killer caught, and they would latch onto anyone who was handy. Fuller did not intend to hang around and be handy. He had spent enough time in this one-horse town anyway. It was time he rejoined the modern world. He finished his packing, but he realized that he couldn't leave with his bag in the daylight. He would go down to the stable and rent a horse, saying that he meant to ride out to see someone in the country. After dark, he would sneak back into the hotel for his bag, sneak out again, and ride out of town, never to return.

Chapter Five

Denver Bond was still waiting in the corner of the upstairs hallway, and he watched as Carl Thurman, the local banker, left the room. Bond felt his throat tighten. If he couldn't overcome this feeling, soon he wouldn't be able to breathe. The door was shut behind Thurman, and the man walked off down the hallway toward the inside stairs. Everyone in the Rattlesnake would know where Thurman had been. Bond's skin felt hot. He knew that he had other things to be doing. He should be out helping Kane with the investigation, but his mind was not on the investigation, and he didn't know what more to do anyway. His mind was on Lottie. When he felt like he had let enough time pass since the departure of Thurman, he walked down to the door. He stood for a moment, his heart beating rapidly, and stared at the door. At last he knocked, very lightly and tentatively. Lottie opened the door.

"Denver," she said, "what are you doing here this

time of day?"

"I just wanted to see you," he said.

"Come in."

She stepped aside, and Bond walked a few feet into the room. His look went directly to the rumpled bed, and he felt like screaming, but he didn't. Instead his hands crunched the brim of the hat he was holding in front of him.

"Is anything wrong?" said Lottie.

"No," said Denver. "No. Nothing's wrong. I just wanted to see you. That's all."

"You know I have to charge you for it this time of day," she said. "I'm on duty."

"That's not why I came," he said. "I just want to talk to you."

"All right," she said. "Sit down."

Bond found a chair and sat in it stiffly, still holding his hat in both hands. Lottie walked over to a table on which were placed several bottles and glasses.

"You want a drink?" she said. "On me."

"Yeah. Thanks," he said.

She poured the drink and took it to him. When he had the drink, she took his hat and hung it on a hat tree which was standing beside the door. Then she poured herself a drink and sat down on the edge of the bed.

"Well?"

"What?" said Bond.

"You said you wanted to talk," she said.

"Oh, yeah."

He took a sip of the warm liquor and waited while it burned its way slowly down to his stomach.

"Lottie," he said, "I want you to quit this business."

"Denver," she said, her voice an admonishment.

"Marry me. I can't stand this," he said. "What you're doing. Knowing about it."

"Denver," she said, "we've been over this before. A dozen times. More than that."

"I got to keep trying," he said. "Maybe you'll change your mind. You can change your mind. Lottie, I love you. You know I do."

"Look," she said. "I've told you before, but I'll say it again. I couldn't take it. There's killers loose in this town. And even before, this has always been a rough town. Drunk cowboys. Brawls. Crooked gamblers. Gunfights. I worry about you enough as it is. If I was married to you, I'd go crazy every day wondering whether or not some drunk cowboy would shoot you down and make me a widow."

"Lottie," Bond said, but she didn't allow him to protest further.

"And besides that," she hurried on, "you wouldn't be able to stand it either. You'd always remember what I'd been. You'd think about all those other men. One day you'd wind up hating me for it."

"I could never hate you, Lottie," he said. "I hate what you're doing, but if you quit, I'll forget all about it. It would just be you and me from then on."

"How could you forget? Everyone in town knows me, knows what I am. They won't let you forget."

Bond stood up and moved toward Lottie.

"Damn it," he said, "I'm scared. You know what's been happening here. Someone's killing—

whores. You could be next. Quit this business. Marry me. You'll be safe then."

Lottie stood up and faced Bond. Her look was stern.

"It's your job and Kane's job to catch that killer," she said, "so do your job, Denver, and keep me safe. Me and all the others. Oh, God, Denver, I'm scared, too. I'm scared all the time, but I'm not going to marry you because I'm scared."

He stepped forward and put his arms around her, and she pressed herself against him. Her arms went around his back.

"I think about them," she said. "Bridgit and Georgia and Mary. I try to remember them the way they used to be, but I can't. All I can see is the way they were after—. I see them dead. I dream about it."

Bond held her tight. He kissed the top of her head. He kissed her cheek and her neck. She turned her face up toward his, and their lips met for a long and passionate kiss.

"I want you, Lottie," he said. "I want you now."

She pulled him toward the bed.

"I won't say anything," she said. "I won't charge you."

Fuller had rented the horse just as he had planned, and he had ridden out to visit with an acquaintance who lived a few miles outside of town. It was the only way he could think of to get his hands on a horse without arousing the suspicion of the sheriff. He felt certain that Kane was watching him, or having him watched. He had spent a casual afternoon visiting, then ridden back to town. The horse was saddled and waiting in front of the hotel. Upstairs in Fuller's room, his bag was packed. He hated to steal the horse, but he didn't want to buy it until he was actually on his way out of town for good, and he didn't want to leave town until well after dark. He finally decided that since Oogene Debs, who owned the stable, lived on the north end of town, he would get his bag and ride by Debs' house, pay him for the horse and then head north. He wondered where he would go. Of course, the main thing was to get out of Jubilation, to get beyond the reach of Sheriff Ben Kane who seemed determined to pin a murder rap on him. But he realized that once he had managed to put a few miles between himself and Jubilation, he would have to have a destination. Dallas, he thought. Dallas was a gambler's town. It was also a safe distance from Jubilation, and it was big enough to get lost in, if a man had a reason to get lost. He would leave just after dark and ride to Dallas.

The closer the stagecoach got to Jubilation, the rougher the road seemed to be, but at least Ellie and Mrs. Higgins had been spared the further close quarter company of Franklin Smith. The driver had very intelligently suggested that Smith ride on top with him and the guard, so inside the coach the Higginses sat together on the backward facing seat, leaving Ellie the entire forward facing one to herself. She would have been glad of that had the ride been smooth, but being alone on the seat, she found that she simply had more room in which to be flung around. She knew that the trip was nearly at its end, yet she was feeling as if it would never end. She was thankful that her pregnancy was no further along. If it had been, she thought, the result would have surely been a miscarriage or at the least a premature birth.

All of a sudden there was a terrific jounce. The right front corner of the coach seemed to have fallen in a hole. Then there was a forward lurch which seemed to bring the corner back up, but not as high up as it had been before. It had a list to the right, and as it moved forward, more slowly than before, there was a maddening grating sound. Mrs. Higgins squealed in fright, and up above the driver shouted at the horses. There was a loud yell and a thump, and finally the coach came to a stop.

"Are you all right?" the driver shouted.

Ellie poked her head out the window to take a look, and she saw Smith flat on his back beside the road some feet behind the stage. He raised up his head and shook it. Then he rolled over on his belly, heaved himself up onto his hands and knees and finally stood up on shaky legs. He looked up toward the driver.

"Yeah," he said. "I'm okay. I think."

The driver set the brake and started climbing down off of the coach.

"Everybody out," he said. "We have an unscheduled rest stop."

Ellie was the first one out of the stage, but the Higgins were close behind her.

"What's happened?" said Higgins.

"Hell," said the driver, "we broke something.

51

Give me a chance to take a look here."

Smith came walking up to join the others, and the guard looked him over carefully as he approached.

"Boy," he said, "you're lucky you didn't break all your bones."

"Yeah," said the driver. "He sure did bounce pretty though, didn't he?"

"Best bounce I ever seen," said the guard.

"Well, what's broken?" said Higgins.

The driver was down on one knee looking under the coach, and the guard was trying to look over his shoulder.

"Thorough brace is busted," said the driver, and he turned around, sat down on the ground and leaned back against the wheel. He reached into his pocket and pulled out a pipe and a tobacco pouch, and he proceeded to fill and light his pipe.

"Well, here now," said Higgins. "What are you going to do about it?"

"Hmm?" said the driver. "Oh. We'll fix her here in a minute."

While he continued to puff at his pipe, the guard climbed back up onto the box and reached down into the front boot. He brought out some tools and spare parts.

"Don't worry, folks," he said. "We'll get you into Jubilation tonight. We'll just be a little later than we expected."

Fuller looked out the window of his hotel room. It was plenty dark outside, and there didn't seem to be many people out on the street. He picked up

52

his bag and left the room. Downstairs in the lobby, he walked over to the counter.

"I'd like to pay my bill," he said.

Tony Arnall looked up from the dime novel he was reading.

"Oh," he said. "You leaving us, Mr. Fuller?"

"Yes," said Fuller. "I'm afraid so."

He placed some bills on the counter, and Arnall made a few quick calculations. He took the bills, produced some change and gave Fuller the change and a copy of the bill.

"Where you headed, Mr. Fuller?" he said.

"I think I'll try El Paso," said Fuller. He felt clever. If Kane questioned Arnall, he would wind up looking in the wrong direction.

"Well, have a good trip, and if you're ever back in Jubilation, be sure to stop in."

"I will, Tony," said Fuller. "Thanks."

He stepped outside and looked up and down the street. It seemed safe enough, so he mounted the rented horse, turned it north and rode slowly toward the edge of town. Just a little ways, he thought. Maybe Kane hasn't even quite made up his mind yet whether or not he wants to arrest me. By the time he decides he does, I'll be half way to Dallas, and by the time he comes after me, I'll be long gone. Up ahead he could see the house of Oogene Debs. His last stop. There was a light on in the house, and Fuller was glad to see that. He hadn't really looked forward to waking up Debs. He rode up to the front of the house and dismounted, tying the horse to a fence rail. Then he walked up to the door and knocked. Debs opened the door from the inside.

"Fuller?" he said.

"Yeah," said Fuller. "Listen, I hate to bother you at home, but you did say that horse was for sale."

"Yeah."

"I want to buy him."

"Now?"

"Now," said Fuller. "I've decided I want to leave town tonight. I've already checked out of my room. I have the exact amount here. Can I pay you for him now?"

"Well," said Debs, "I guess so. I'll just have to get a paper and pencil and write you out a bill of sale."

Debs disappeared back into the house, and Fuller waited anxiously for a few moments. Then Debs came back out. Fuller paid him and took the bill of sale.

"Thanks," he said.

"Sure," said Debs. "Business is business."

He closed the door, and Fuller walked back to his horse. He unwrapped the reins from the rail and stuck his left foot into the stirrup. He was about to swing up into the saddle when he heard the voice behind him.

"Hold it right there, Fuller."

The next sound Fuller heard was the unmistakeable metallic click-click of the cocking of a single-action revolver. He dropped his foot back to the ground, slowly rewrapped the reins around the rail and raised his hands over his head. Then he turned to look into the barrel of a Colt .44 held in the right hand of Sheriff Ben Kane.

"Let's go," said Kane.

"Where, may I ask?" said Fuller.

"Jailhouse. You're under arrest for murder."

When the stagecoach finally rolled into Jubilation, the town looked dead. There was no one in the street, and there were few lights. Ellie disembarked and stood on the sidewalk, her bag in her hand, uncertain what to do next.

"Excuse me," said Franklin Smith.

Ellie turned her face away from Smith.

"I know what you think of me," he said. "I think that I must have been suffering from stagecoach craziness. I've been traveling for too long. Is your fiance going to meet you here?"

"No," she said. "He—doesn't know exactly when to expect me."

"Do you have a place to stay?"

"I'll need a hotel," said Ellie.

"I'm going to the hotel," said Smith. "I can walk you there. I won't touch you. I won't even get close. Look."

He pointed down the street.

"It's just there," he said. "Well, I'm going on."

Smith started walking toward the hotel, and Ellie waited a moment, then followed. She stayed a few paces behind the man. She could see that it was a hotel he had pointed at, and the others from the stage were still within easy shouting distance. It should be safe enough.

Chapter Six

Ellie had thought that she would be up and about early looking for Richard Fuller, but she surprised herself by sleeping half the morning away. It had been a long and tiring trip, and she had slept but fitfully all the way. After a bath, the first she had been able to take since leaving the ranch, and a change into fresh clothes, she felt much better. She was refreshed, rested and ready to go on her search. Then for the first time since her original decision to find Fuller and marry him, she began to feel serious doubts. He might not even be in Jubilation. He might have left without telling anyone where he was going, and she might never see him again. But even if she did find him, what would she say to him? How would she approach him? She had been so determined, so resolute. Now she felt like a helpless fool. She felt like crying. But she had not done that yet, and she had no intention of doing it now. She stepped in front of the mirror in the hotel room and looked at herself. Her clothes were rumpled from having been crammed into the traveling bag, and she really didn't think that she looked particularly appealing. She opened her purse and counted her money. She had plenty, she thought. Yet she didn't know how long it would have to last her. She decided to take a chance. She needed to look just right. She needed a new outfit. She put the money back in the purse and went downstairs.

"Good morning, Miss," said Tony Arnall. "I hope you rested up from your trip all right."

"Quite nicely, thank you," said Ellie. "I wonder if you could answer some questions for me?"

"I'll do my best."

"I need to buy some new clothes. Can you suggest a place?"

"There's a dry goods store just across the street," said Arnall. And there's a dressmaker right next door to it."

"Thank you."

It would be foolish to spend her money on a new dress and then find out that Fuller was not in town, she thought.

"Do you know Mr. Richard Fuller?" she asked.

"Sure," said Arnall. "He stayed right here. In fact, his room was the one right next to yours."

"Was?" said Ellie.

"He just checked out last night," said Arnall.

"Oh, I see," said Ellie. She tried not to let her disappointment show to the hotel clerk. "Did he happen to mention where he was going?"

"Matter of fact, he did," said Arnall. "Told me

he was going to El Paso. He said he thought that was a good town for a gambler."

"But how did he leave?" said Ellie. "Was there a stage out last night going that direction?"

"Oh, he never made it, Miss," said Arnall. "The sheriff caught him on his way out of town and put him in jail."

"In jail," said Ellie. "Whatever for?"

Arnall eyed Ellie with sudden curiosity.

"Uh, excuse me, Miss," he said. "I'm sure it's none of my business, but, if you don't mind saying, just what is Mr. Fuller to you?"

"I came here to marry Mr. Fuller," said Ellie.

Arnall sighed heavily.

"Well," he said, "I'm real sorry to be the one to have to tell you this, but you'll have to find it out one way or another."

"What?" said Ellie.

"If you mean to marry Fuller," said Arnall, "you'd best hurry up and get it done. I expect they're going to hang him."

Ellie's jaw dropped, and her eyes opened wide. She stared at Arnall, and her face went deathly pale. She couldn't have heard him right, she thought. She just couldn't have. Not after she had come all this way. Not in the condition she was in. To find him in jail. And condemned. It just couldn't be possible.

"But," she stammered, "but why? What—what is he supposed to have done?"

"They say he killed a man, Miss," said Arnall. "I'm sorry."

Ellie took a deep breath trying to regain her

composure. She stood up straight and as tall as she could, and she looked Arnall directly in the eyes.

"Where is the sheriff's office?" she said.

"Go straight across the street to the dry goods store," said Arnall, "turn to your left. It's two doors down."

"Thank you," she said, and she turned and walked out the door. Standing on the sidewalk, she looked across the street and to her left. She could see the sheriff's office. A cowboy was riding down the street, and she waited for him to pass her by, then she hurried across and down to the sheriff's door. She opened the door and stepped boldly inside. It was small office with one large desk and one small desk. Each desk had a chair, and there were two extra straight-backed chairs in the room. On one wall was a gun rack. In a corner was a pot-bellied stove with a coffee pot sitting on top of it. On the back wall there was a heavy door with a small barred window. That must lead to the cells, she thought. Richard is back there somewhere. Ben Kane looked up from behind his desk as Ellie shut the front door behind herself.

"You must be the sheriff," said Ellie.

"I'm Sheriff Ben Kane, ma'am," said Kane, standing up behind his desk. "Is there something I can do for you?"

"My name is Ellie McKee. I understand you have a Mr. Richard Fuller in your custody. Is that correct?"

"Yes, ma'am," said Kane. "That is correct."

"May I know what it is he is charged with?"

"It's murder," said Kane.

"Is there any question regarding Mr. Fuller's guilt?"

"Not in my mind, there isn't," said Kane. "But then, I'm not the one to make that determination. That'll be up to a jury."

"May I know the circumstances of the crime?"

"Well, now, I don't know, Miss," said Kane, walking out from behind his desk and studying Ellie as he walked. "I never saw you before in my life. I think you're a stranger here. You must have come in on that stage last night. Did you?"

"Yes," said Ellie. "I did."

"So you come in here asking all kinds of questions about an arrest I only made last night. I've got to wonder just what your interest is, lady."

"So you won't tell me the circumstances of the killing? Why you arrested Mr. Fuller?"

"Not unless you tell me something first," said Kane. He picked a cup up off of his desk and walked to the pot-bellied stove. There he poured himself a cup of coffee. "Would you like some coffee?" he said.

"No, thank you," said Ellie. "If you must know, Sheriff, I came to town with the intention of marrying Mr. Fuller. I only this morning found out that he had been arrested."

"Oh, I see," said Kane. He walked back around behind his desk and sat down, placing the cup on the desk in front of him. "Well, my advice is to forget about him and go on back home. You see he was in a poker game with a man called Coker Jack. Fuller lost and he accused Coker Jack of cheating. He and Jack drew guns on each other,

60

but no shots were fired. That same night, Coker Jack was beat to death with an ax handle and robbed of all his money. I arrested your Mr. Fuller late last night trying to sneak out of town."

"So the evidence is all circumstantial," said Ellie. "He might not be guilty."

"I wouldn't count on that, little lady," said Kane.

"May I see him?" said Ellie. "Please."

"Uh, Miss—. What did you say your name is?"

"Ellie McKee."

"Miss McKee," said Kane, "take my advice. Forget Fuller. Go on back home, wherever that is. You'll be a whole lot better off, believe me. One day you'll look back, and you'll see that I'm right."

"Sheriff," said Ellie, "I must see Mr. Fuller."

Kane fell back in his chair and heaved a sigh. He stared at Ellie for a moment. Then he opened a desk drawer and took out a ring of keys. He stood up and headed for the heavy door on the back wall.

"Come on," he said.

He unlocked the door and opened it, and as he did, the hinges creaked. Behind the door was a long, dark hallway with cells on either side.

"Fuller," shouted Kane, "are you decent?"

"Decent?" came Fuller's voice from down the hall. "Of course I am. That's more than I can say for my surroundings though."

"Shut up," said Kane. "You've got a visitor. A young lady."

"What?" said Fuller. "A young lady? Who?"

"He's in the last cell on the left, Miss," said Kane. "Go ahead. I'll leave this door open to give you a little more light."

"Thank you," said Ellie, and she started walking down the dark corridor.

In the far cell, Richard Fuller had stood up. He was shoving his shirt tail down into his trousers and pressing his face between the bars in an attempt to see who it was who had come to see him. But the hallway was dark, and the female figure he saw approaching was moving slowly, slowly and deliberately. There was something familiar in the shape, in the way she moved. She took another step, and suddenly he could see her clearly. He pressed his face harder into the bars. He saw her, but he didn't believe what he was seeing. It just wasn't possible. It made no sense. It—.

"Ellie?" he said.

"Richard," she said, "did you kill that man?"

"No, I didn't kill him. I've never killed anyone in my whole life."

"I'm glad," she said. "I believe you. I didn't really think that you had done it."

"But what are you doing here?" he said. "How did you get here? Why?"

"I came looking for you," she said. "I got your letter."

"Oh, Ellie," he said. "You shouldn't have come. I only wrote to you because I didn't want to hurt you. Well, I guess I already hurt you, but I didn't want to hurt you worse. I'm no good for you. Can't you see that?"

"You said that you love me," she said.

"Yes," he said. "I did. I think I did say that."

"Was it a lie?"

"No, it wasn't a lie. It was—. Well, I think what I said was that I love you in my own way."

"Your own 'peculiar' way," Ellie corrected.

"Yes."

"And I love you. I told you that."

"Yes, I know you did, but—."

"Then it's all very simple, isn't it?" said Ellie. "I love you and you love me. And now I'm here."

"Yeah," said Fuller. "You're here. Just how did you get here, anyway?"

"Oh, that was easy," she said. "I rode Sampson into town, sold him and bought a railroad ticket. I took the train as far south as it would bring me, and then I rode a stage on down here. I got in late last night and got a room in the hotel. This morning, the man in the hotel told me where to find you."

"I guess it's all over town by now," he said.

"Probably," said Ellie.

"Well, you're going to have to go back home," he said. "Have you got enough money to get back?"

"That's what the sheriff told me," she said. "To go back home. I'm not going."

Fuller put both hands to his head in frustration and began pacing his small cell.

"Ellie," he said, "your folks must be worried to death."

"I wrote them a letter and told them not to worry. I told them what I was up to."

"That's great," said Fuller. "Now if I ever get out of this mess I'm in, your father will come down here and kill me."

"No, he won't," said Ellie. "I didn't tell him

where I would be. Would you stop that?"

"What?"

"That pacing. Will you stop it please and come over here and talk to me?"

Fuller walked back to the bars. He gripped two bars with his hands and looked hard into Ellie's face.

"Ellie," he said, "please listen to me. You have to go home. I may never get out of here. They might even hang me. You don't need to be here for that."

"That sheriff does seem pretty convinced that you'll be found guilty," said Ellie, "but as he himself pointed out to me, he's not the jury. And all his evidence is circumstantial."

"Ellie," said Fuller, his voice full of protest.

"Richard, I came here to get married."

"Wha—? What?"

"I came here to marry you," she said. "You didn't think that I traveled all that distance just to say hello, did you?"

"But—but I told you in my letter why that would never work, and now it's worse than ever. There's no future in marrying a man who's going on trial for murder."

Ellie ducked her head and looked at the floor.

"I had hoped that you'd be happy to see me," she said. "I hoped that when you saw me, you'd change your mind about what you wrote. I even hoped that maybe by the time I got here, you would have already changed your mind. At the very least, I had hoped that I wouldn't have to tell you what I'm going to tell you now."

"What are you talking about?" said Fuller.

"Richard," she said, and she looked up again, looked into his eyes. "Richard, I'm going to have a baby, and it's your baby. So you see, I have to marry you, whether you get out of here or not. I have to have your name. Our baby has to have your name. I'll not have our baby going through life being called—a bastard."

Fuller stared at Ellie for a long moment. Then he turned and walked over to the cot against the wall, and he sat down heavily on its edge, his head in his hands. He lifted his head to look again at Ellie.

"Oh, God," he said. "Well, yeah. Sure. Of course, I'll marry you—if they'll let me."

"You just leave all that to me, Richard," said Ellie. "I'll be back."

And she turned and walked back down the long, dark corridor and disappeared out the door. Fuller was still staring after her when Kane slammed the heavy door shut and locked it from the other side.

Chapter Seven

Ellie stopped in the sheriff's office on her way out. Kane, having relocked the big door, went back behind his desk and replaced the key ring in the desk drawer. He sat down again. Ellie was standing in the middle of the room.

"Well," he said, "are you satisfied now?"

"I'm satisfied that Mr. Fuller is innocent of the charges you've made," said Ellie.

"Well, little lady," said Kane, "that's not for you or me to decide now."

"No, it isn't," said Ellie. "When will the trial be held?"

"The circuit judge is due to be in Jubilation in about two weeks, Miss McKee," said Kane. "We'll try him then."

"Circuit judge?" said Ellie. "You actually still have a circuit judge?"

"Towns in this part of the state are few and far between," said Kane. "Even when you find one, it's small. Not too many people. Yes, ma'am. We still make use of a circuit judge. You might think we're backward here in some ways, but then, you can always go back home. Can't you?"

"Yes," said Ellie. "Well, in that case, Mr. Fuller and I must be married right away. Will you agree to allow that?"

"Young woman," said Kane, "do your parents know what you're doing?"

"I am of age," said Ellie.

"I don't suppose it would do any good for me to offer more advice?"

"My mind is made up, Sheriff."

"What do you want to marry a murderer for?" said Kane. "A man that's going to be hanged?"

"That determination has yet to be made," said Ellie. "You yourself just reminded me of that."

"Yes, ma'am," said Kane, "but the odds are pretty strong against him. And even if it should go his way, he's a gambler. A footloose, professional cardsharp. The worst thing you could do to yourself is to get hooked up with a man like that. He'd make a misery of your life."

"But you think the odds are strong that he won't be around long enough to make a misery of my life," said Ellie.

"You want to be a young widow?"

"Sheriff," said Ellie, "will you allow the wedding or not?"

"No, by God, I will not," said Kane. "It's for your own good."

"Very well," she said, sitting down. "I'll have to tell you the whole story. If the worst should happen, and Mr. Fuller is convicted and hanged, that

67

only makes a quick wedding the more necessary. You see, Sheriff, I'm going to have his child. So I need his name."

Kane cleared his throat and shifted his weight in his chair. He leaned an elbow on his desk and put a hand to his forehead. With the fingers of his other hand, he drummed the desk top. Finally he leaned back again in his chair and looked at Ellie.

"Gospel Bill," he said.

"I beg your pardon," said Ellie.

"That's the man you want. He's the only one around. Reverend William Varner. We call him Gospel Bill."

"Where might I find Reverend Varner?" said Ellie.

"Go clean down to the south end of the street," said Kane. "Turn to your left. You'll see a big canvas tent. Like a circus tent. That's Gospel Bill's church. It's also his house. If you don't find him there, he's apt to be preaching in the street somewhere, most likely in front of a saloon."

"Thank you," said Ellie. She stood up to leave.

"Just let me know when to expect the wedding," Kane said as Ellie was opening the door.

"I will," she said, and she went outside and turned south. She found the tent without any trouble. Kane might have exaggerated, but only slightly. The tent might have been large enough to accommodate a small circus, one ring only. It was old and dirty and weather-beaten. The door flaps were down but not secured. Ellie pushed one flap aside and stuck her head in.

"Hello," she said. "Reverend Varner? Are you in?"

At the far end of the tent was a simple, plain pulpit. Between Ellie and the pulpit were two rows of rough wooden benches.

"Hello," she called again.

Then she heard a coughing and a spluttering from back behind the pulpit. Finally the voice formed understandable words.

"Ye have heard of the patience of Job?" it said. "Therefore be patient. Hold your horses, and I'll be with you in a minute."

Ellie stretched her neck and squinted her eyes in the direction of the pulpit, and she saw a figure rise up from behind that holy rostrum. It seemed to be shrouded and somewhat shaggy, and it shook itself for a moment before its disheveled head turned to face her. As her eyes became adjusted to the dim interior of the tent, Ellie could see that the figure was that of a tall and lank man with white hair and gaunt features. He was wrapped in a blanket that appeared to be of U.S. Army issue. He shrugged the blanket off his shoulders, allowing it to drop to the ground at his feet. Underneath the blanket he had been fully dressed. His black suit, topped off with a long frock coat, was worn and frayed and rumpled. The old man stepped out from behind the pulpit and started walking down the aisle toward where Ellie waited. As he came closer, Ellie could see that blades of grass were stuck in his hair and to his clothing.

"I've been napping," he said. "For we which have believed do enter into rest, as he said. Hello. I don't believe I know you."

"My name is Ellie McKee," said Ellie. "I've only just arrived in town."

"Welcome, my child, to this, my temple in the wilderness. I am the Reverend William Varner at your service. What can I do for you? Seek and ye shall find. Ask and it shall be given to you. Knock and the door shall be opened unto you. What do you want?"

"I want you to perform a wedding, Reverend," said Ellie.

"Ah," said Varner, "I speak this by permission and not of commandment. For I would that all men were even as I myself, and I say therefore to the unmarried and widows, it is good for them if they abide even as I."

"Reverend Varner, I must be married," said Ellie, "and soon."

"But if they cannot contain," said Varner, "let them marry: for it is better to marry than to burn. Who is the man? When and where is the wedding to be held?"

"My fiance is Mr. Richard Fuller," said Ellie. "The wedding must be held in the jail, as Mr. Fuller is presently incarcerated there. Tomorrow would be ideal. That would give me time to buy a new dress and Mr. Fuller time to prepare himself."

"It shall be so," said the Reverend.

"Would ten o'clock in the morning be convenient?"

"Let every one of us please his neighbor," said Varner. "At ten o'clock I'll meet you in the pokey."

Richard Fuller stood at the bars for a long time after Ellie left him. Finally he went back to the cot and sat down. The seeming unreality of the scene

that had just transpired overwhelmed him. At last
he began to consider the enormity of the commit-
ment he had just made. My God, he thought, I've
just consented to marry the girl. What if they don't
hang me? I'll be stuck with a wife. He asked himself how it had all come about. He wondered what
he had done to deserve all that was happening to
him. He had been arrested for murder and was
likely to hang, but even if he beat the murder
charge, he was going to wind up with a life sen-
tence. He could hardly believe that Ellie had managed to follow him all the way to Jubilation, Texas.
She was just a — a girl. And of course he had taken
advantage of her. He was lucky he had not been
killed by J.W. McKee. Of course, that would have
saved him from both the hangman and the wedding. He couldn't quite decide where the luck was
in the overall situation.

And he couldn't quite blame old McKee. If he
had been in the man's place, he thought, he would
certainly have murdered the man who had taken
advantage of his young and innocent daughter. He
would —. Just then he was struck by a new and
astonishing thought. He could wind up in the same
position as McKee. He was going to be a father. It
could easily turn out to be a girl. He wondered if
it would be a girl or a boy. He wondered how it
would turn out, what kind of life it would have,
and then he wondered if he would ever know. He
wondered if he would live to see it. Well, he
thought, at least it would have his name. But then
that thought was not particularly comforting. What
sort of person would it grow into? Who was going
to be walking around the world presenting itself as

his offspring, using his name? He would have no control over that. Not if he had been hanged.

"Richard Fuller," he said out loud, "you damned fool. What the hell have you gotten yourself into this time?"

He stood up and paced the floor of the small cell. Down at the end of the hall the big door creaked on its hinges, and soon Fuller could see Denver Bond approaching with his noon meal on a tray.

"Brought your lunch," said Bond. Fuller sat back down on the cot while Bond slid the tray under the bars. It was a house rule that Fuller had already learned.

"Thanks," said Fuller.

"It don't look bad today," said Bond.

Fuller picked up his tray and took it back to the cot to sit down and eat.

"Say," said Bond, "I hear there's going to be a wedding."

"It, uh, it looks that way," said Fuller, without enthusiasm.

"Be a first," said Bond.

"What?"

"We've never had a wedding in the jailhouse before. It'll be a first."

"Oh," said Fuller.

"She seems like an awful nice lady," said Bond. "Real pretty, too. You're a lucky man."

Fuller had a mouthful of food, and in response to Bond's last remark, he just looked up at the deputy.

"Well," said Bond, "in a manner of speaking, that is. Say, Fuller?"

"Yeah?"

"I've been wanting to tell you, I never thought you done that killing. I still don't think it. 'Course, what I think don't make a hell of a lot of difference. But, well, for what it's worth."

"Thanks, Denver," said Fuller. "I wish your boss felt the same way."

"Yeah. Well, happy wedding, Fuller. I'll be back in a while for the tray."

"Hey, Denver."

"Yeah?"

"Will you be here for the wedding?"

"You want me to be here?"

"Yeah."

"Well, by God, I will be then. Thank you. I'll see you again in a few minutes. Sheriff's out, and I've got to watch the front."

"Okay," said Fuller. He was surprised at how hungry he was, and in a few minutes he had cleaned the tray. He shoved it under the bars back out into the hallway, and he went back to his cot.

"Married," he said out loud. "A father."

Denver Bond had been right about one thing, he thought. Ellie was nice—and pretty. But she was more than that. She was one damn determined young woman. Suddenly Fuller was proud of Ellie. Not many women would have done what she had done. She had traveled alone a long distance to find him and to—to make him marry her. Did it ever occur to Ellie that he might simply have refused her? Some scoundrels would under the same circumstances. She was bright, she was pretty, she was spunky. She had been a great lover. And she was rich. Well, her father was rich. Fuller slowly came to the conclusion that there were lots of worse things in this world than marriage to Ellie, and the more he thought about it, the more he was convinced that he did not want to hang.

Out in the office, Denver Bond walked to the window and looked out onto the street. He could see the Rattlesnake from where he stood, and he imagined that he could see the room upstairs where his Lottie plied her trade. He felt an aching inside, a dull sickness of the heart or of the soul, and he thought about the ironies of life, even though he did not know that word. He thought about the woman across the street who refused to marry him, the woman he loved and wanted in spite of her profession, the woman he would cross an ocean to marry. He had begged her, and still she refused. He poured out his love to her, and she said no. He humiliated himself before her, and still she wouldn't budge. He promised her protection from the mysterious killer, and she was afraid for her life, yet still she would not give in.

And then he thought of the young woman who had traveled far and alone to force herself on Fuller. Fuller was a professional gambler, a footloose rambler. At the moment, he was also a jailbird and an accused murderer with a very uncertain future. And he was about to be married in his jail cell. Bond thought that Fuller was a very lucky man indeed. He thought that he would happily change places with Fuller if he could. That is, he would die happy, if only he could first marry Lottie. No, he did not know the word irony, but he knew too well the human condition that the word designated, and he felt its bite.

Ellie was pleased to discover that Jubilation was not behind the times when it came to ladies' fashions. The latest styles had reached even the most remote corners of the country apparently. Most likely that was attributable to the Montgomery Ward and Sears and Roebuck mail order catalogues that seemed to be able to find everyone these days. She was leaving the dressmaker's shop with her new dress when she saw Sheriff Ben Kane walking toward the Rattlesnake Saloon. She crossed the street just in time to intercept him.

"Sheriff Kane," she said. "I found Reverend Varner."

"Good," said Kane.

"He's coming to the jail in the morning at ten o'clock. Is that all right?"

"If you're determined to go through with this," said Kane, "I suppose that's as good a time as any."

"Would you please tell Mr. Fuller?"

"Yes, ma'am. I'll tell him."

"Thank you, Sheriff," said Ellie, and she went on her way back to the hotel. Kane resumed his walk to the Rattlesnake. He pushed open the swinging door and went inside. He didn't have to look far to find the person he was looking for. Donald Kane was sitting alone with a bottle of whiskey and a glass. The sheriff walked over to the table.

"Donnie," he said.

"Please, Father," said the younger Kane. "Donald. I think I've outgrown the diminutive."

"I'm sorry, Donald," said Kane. "Don't you think it's a bit early in the day for that?"

"Don't nag, Father. Please."

"I don't mean to, but I worry about you, Son. Will you be home early tonight? I'll fix up a real good supper."

"I don't know, Father. I just don't know. Don't wait up. Okay?"

"Donald."

Donald Kane poured his glass full of whiskey and held it up toward his father as if for a toast. Then he drank it down in a gulp.

Chapter Eight

"Hey, there's going to be a wedding down at the jailhouse," Oogene Debs shouted. He had just burst through the front doors of the Rattlesnake Saloon. The few customers in the Rattlesnake at this early hour, mostly cowboys, the three or four working girls in the place, and the bartender all ran for the door. On his way out the bartender locked the doors and hung up the "Closed" sign. Debs was already halfway to the jail, and he was shouting the news all along the street. People walking down the sidewalks and riding horses down the street followed. One young man on a bicycle going the other direction stopped, dismounted, turned his bicycle around and started up again, joining the flow of the crowd. It was as if someone had yelled, "Fire."

At the jail, Gospel Bill had already made his appearance. He was wearing his black suit, rumpled as usual, with bits of grass still stuck to it here and there. His white hair stuck out from his head in all directions, and he clutched in his right hand a worn and tattered Bible. He was standing in the office, facing Ben Kane, who was sitting behind his desk.

"We'll go back to the cell and get this over with," said Kane, "just as soon as the girl shows up."

The heavy door which led to the cells was standing open. Down at the end of the hallway, Denver Bond was beside the cell in which Richard Fuller waited.

"Turn around here," Bond was saying. "Let me see."

Inside the cell, Fuller, with his back to Bond, was straightening his coat. He turned around to face Bond through the bars.

"How's that?" he said.

"That's fine," said Bond. "You look just fine. How do you feel?"

"I'm all right," said Fuller. "Just a little nervous maybe. I wish you had a bottle of whiskey with you. I could use a drink."

"It's against the rules," said Bond.

"I know," said Fuller. "How about a smoke?"

"I didn't know you smoked, Fuller," said Bond.

"I don't," said Fuller. "Usually. How about it?"

"What?"

"Do you have a smoke?"

"Oh. Well, let me see. I don't smoke either. You want me to go find one?"

"No. Never mind."

Fuller was pacing the floor all this time, and he continued to pace.

"Miss Ellie ought to be getting here any minute

now," said Bond. "Old Gospel Bill is out there with the sheriff already. Hell, boy, we'll have you hitched here before you know it."

"Yeah," said Fuller. "I know it."

"Can't you stand still?"

"No. Can you go find me a smoke?"

Out in the office, Kane stood up and began to pace the floor.

"That girl ought to be here," he said.

"Patience is a virtue," said Gospel Bill. "Be therefore both patient and virtuous."

"I know. I know," said Kane. Then he heard the noise out in the street. "What's that?"

He started for the door, but the door burst open just as Bond came into the office from the other door. Debs stepped in from the outside.

"It ain't over yet, is it?" he said.

The door was jammed with others trying to crowd their way in.

"What are you doing here?" demanded Kane.

"We come to see the wedding," said Debs. "It ain't over, is it?"

"No," said Kane, "but you're not coming in here. Get out."

An uproar came from the crowd, and it became obvious to Kane that what he could see crowded in the doorway was just a small portion of those who had gathered. Gospel Bill stood silent with a little sly grin on his wrinkled old face. Kane raised his arms in an attempt to silence the din. When he finally got some quiet, he made a quick decision followed by a declaration.

79

"The wedding will take place outside," he said. "Get everybody out in the street, and get some order. Now go on."

Debs took charge and shoved and shooed the crowd backwards into the street. Bond followed and bummed a ready roll cigarette off a man in the crowd and headed back for Fuller's cell with it. Gospel Bill waited a few minutes to allow Debs time to gain control over the crowd. Then he sidled up to Debs.

"Brother Oogene," he said, "get the men all to one side and the women to the other. And make them leave an aisle down the center. This here is a solemn and holy occasion, and let's see to it that the multitude has got the proper spirit."

It took awhile, but the crowd was at last organized. The people stood in two groups, one male, the other female, in the street facing the sheriff's office. They stood in neat rows, and between the two groups was an aisle of maybe five feet in width. Gospel Bill and Sheriff Kane stood on the board sidewalk looking over the crowd. A couple of cowboys who had come from the Rattlesnake Saloon had carried their bottles with them, but under the stern gaze of Gospel Bill with the added terrestrial authority of the sheriff standing beside him, they discreetly held their bottles behind their backs.

Back at the cell, Bond held a match through the bars from which Fuller could light his smoke. Fuller took a deep draw to light the ready roll and coughed from the sudden rush of powerful smoke.

Then he held the cigarette out away from himself and looked at it accusingly.

"Pretty strong?" said Bond.

"No," said Fuller. "It's good. Damn good."

He took another drag. This time he was ready for it, and he only coughed a little.

"Let me try it," said Bond.

Fuller handed the cigarette to Bond, who took a timid little puff. The smoke never reached his lungs.

"That's not the way to do it," said Fuller.

"What?" said Bond, looking as if his manhood had just been challenged.

"Take a real draw on it," said Fuller. "You've got to inhale the smoke. Get a lung full of it."

"I know that," said Bond. He put the cigarette back to his lips and sucked at it deeply, and the smoke came back out in an explosive cough.

"That's the way," said Fuller. "Here. Let me have it back."

Bond handed the cigarette back to Fuller and coughed a few more times.

"Hey, Denver," said Fuller. "Would you go see what's happening out there?"

"Sure."

Bond started down the hallway. About halfway to the door, he stopped and called back over his shoulder to Fuller.

"I'll be right back," he said.

Fuller continued to pace the floor of the tiny cell and to puff on the ready roll.

When Bond got back to the office, he found it

empty, so he stepped out onto the sidewalk. He stopped and stood there for a moment mesmerized. He was like a man who had inadvertently stepped out onto a stage in front of an audience, and he suffered from a moment of intense stagefright. Then he saw Ellie.

"Here she comes," he shouted.

The crowd turned to look, and a general cheer rose up. Ellie, in her new dress, was walking down the sidewalk on the opposite side of the street. Kane turned to Bond.

"Go get the prisoner," he said. "And bring a pair of handcuffs."

"Handcuffs?" said Bond.

"You heard me. Do it."

Bond went inside, as Gospel Bill stepped center stage.

"My friends," he roared out suddenly, "we're gathered here for a solemn occasion. We're here to witness the union in the sight of God of a man and a woman in holy matrimony."

He looked across the street where Ellie had just come in line with the aisle between the two groups of spectators.

"Just keep on a coming, sister," he said. "That's right. Right through there."

Ellie felt her face flush slightly. She had not expected such a scene. But she maintained her composure and started walking down the aisle.

"Know ye not," roared Gospel Bill, "that the unrighteous shall not inherit the Kingdom of God? Be not deceived: neither fornicators, nor idolaters, nor effeminate, nor abusers of themselves with mankind.

"Nor thieves, nor covetous, nor drunkards, nor revilers, nor extortioners, shall inherit the kingdom of God.

"And such were some of you: but ye are washed, but ye are sanctified, but ye are justified in the name of the Lord Jesus, and by the spirit of our God."

Bond stepped out onto the sidewalk with Richard Fuller. He held in his hands a pair of handcuffs. Kane moved quickly. He took the cuffs from Bond and guided Fuller over to one of the posts which held up the roof which projected out over the sidewalk. He hooked Fuller's hands together around the post. Fuller looked out over the crowd, and he saw Ellie coming down the aisle. His eyes met hers, and she stopped for just an instant before continuing on her way. Gospel Bill had paused in his sermon while these distractions were taking place, but as soon as the bridegroom had been secured, he resumed, his voice stronger than ever.

"All things are lawful unto me," he said, "but all things are not expedient: all things are lawful for me, but I will not be brought under the power of any.

"Meats for the belly, and the belly for meats: but God shall destroy both it and them. Now the body is not for fornication, but for the Lord; and the Lord for the body.

"Know ye not that your bodies are the members of Christ? Shall I then take the members of Christ, and make them the members of a harlot? God forbid.

"But he that is joined unto the Lord is one spirit.

"Flee fornication. Every sin that a man doeth is without the body; but he that committeth fornication sinneth against his own body.

"What? Know ye not that your body is the temple of the Holy Ghost, which is in you, which ye have of God, and ye are not your own?

"For ye are bought with a price: therefore glorify God in your body, and in your spirit, which are God's."

During all this long sermon, Gospel Bill had been stalking back and forth across the board sidewalk, which had become his stage, in front of his audience. He had almost worn himself out, and he stopped to take several deep breaths. Then he looked over his congregation dramatically. Ellie was standing in the street there in front of him. He reached down toward her.

"Step up here, my child," he said, "and take your place beside your betrothed."

Ellie did as the preacher told her to do, but the post which held Richard Fuller captive was between her and him. Still she held his hands in hers.

"Nevertheless," shouted Gospel Bill, "to avoid fornication, let every man have his own wife, and let every woman have her own husband.

"For I would that all men were even as I myself, and I say therefore to the unmarried and widows, it is good for them if they abide even as I.

"But if they cannot contain, let them marry: for it is better to marry than to burn."

Then Gospel Bill stopped and stood up straight before the gathered crowd. He held both arms up over his head and stood there for a moment in silence. When he resumed speaking, it was without his previous animation.

"Dearly beloved," he intoned, "we are gathered here together in the sight of God to witness the joining together into one flesh this man and this woman in holy matrimony, which is an honorable estate. If there be anyone here who knows of any reason wherefore this marriage should not take place, let him speak now or forever hold his tongue. Seeing no one come forward, we shall proceed."

He turned to Fuller.

"Do you have a ring?"

Fuller stammered, and Lottie stepped forward from the women's side of the congregation. She pulled a gold ring off her finger and put it in Fuller's hand.

"It's better by far to give than to receive," said Gospel Bill. "Thank you, my child. Now do you—? What's your name?"

"Richard Fuller."

"Do you Richard Fuller take this woman to be your lawful wedded wife? If you do, say I do."

"I do," said Fuller, and he felt a lump in his throat. He wondered if the hangman's rope would eventually squeeze it out.

"And do you—. What's your name again, my dear?"

"Ellie McKee."

"Do you Ellie McKee take this man to be your lawful wedded husband? If you do, say I do."

"I do," said Ellie.

"Put the ring on her finger," said Gospel Bill, and Fuller managed to do that. "Now," the preacher continued, "by the authority vested in me by the great and sovereign state of Texas and by Almighty God, I pronounce you to be man and wife, one flesh, and if you must, you may now kiss the bride."

Ellie stepped up close so that Fuller could kiss her. She put an arm around his shoulders, but he, of course, could do nothing toward an embrace. He was already embracing the post. As their lips met, Gospel Bill shouted, "Amen," and a great cheer rose up from the crowd. As soon as the noise subsided a bit, Sheriff Kane took over center stage.

"The show's over, folks," he shouted. "Break it up and go on about your business."

He turned to find his deputy.

"Take him back in, Denver," he said.

Bond unlocked the cuffs and led Fuller, looking over his shoulder at Ellie, back into the jail. The crowd began breaking up. Ellie handed a crumpled bill to the preacher.

"Thank you," she said.

"Tis better to give than to receive," he said. "Praise the Lord."

Ellie looked around. She saw the woman who had donated the ring walking away, and she hurried to overtake her.

"Excuse me," she said.

Lottie stopped walking and turned back to face Ellie. Ellie pulled the ring off her finger.

"Thank you very much for the use of the ring," she said.

"Oh," said Lottie, "that's all right. You keep it, honey. It's your wedding ring."

"But I can't just take your ring," said Ellie.

"I wouldn't feel right taking it back," said Lottie.

"That is, unless you feel like it's, well, demeaning or something."

"Oh, no. Why would I think that?"

Lottie cocked her head and looked at Ellie, as if trying to figure out something about her.

"You mean," she said, "you don't know what I am?"

"Why, no," said Ellie. "I don't believe I've ever seen you before. Have I?"

"I guess not. I'm a whore, honey. Plain and simple. Now do you want to wear the ring?"

"Yes," said Ellie. "I do. I'd like for Richard to buy me a ring one of these days, if he can, but until he does, I'd like very much to wear this one. I'd also like to have lunch with you, unless you have other plans."

"No," said Lottie. "I don't have any plans for lunch. Come on. I know a good place."

Chapter Nine

"I'm Ellie McKee," said Ellie, offering her hand. "I mean, I'm Ellie Fuller. I'll have to get used to that."

Lottie took the hand.

"I'm Lottie Kuntz," she said. "I'm glad to make your acquaintance. Do you like good Mexican food?"

"I love it," said Ellie, "but, uh, I don't think I should have any just now. Something plainer, I think."

"Okay," said Lottie. "We'll go down here to Bubba's. You can't get food any plainer than his. It's good food. It's just not very imaginative."

The two women walked off down the street together, and Denver Bond stepped out of the front door of the sheriff's office to watch them. The one woman had just gotten married. The other Bond wanted desperately to wed for himself. And the ring of his beloved was on the finger of the other.

It had just been used in a marriage ceremony. Oh, God, he said to himself. What do I have to do? What's going to happen to me? What'll become of her?

Kane stepped out of the office.

"I'm going to the house for awhile, Denver," he said. "Keep an eye on things here. Will you?"

"Sure, Ben."

Kane walked away, and Bond stayed there beside the door for a few more minutes. He saw Oogene Debs walking in his direction.

"Oogene," he said. "You got a couple of minutes? Will you do me a favor?"

"Sure," said Debs. "What do you need?"

Bond dug into his pocket and pulled out some coins. He handed the money to Debs.

"Would you run over to the Rattlesnake and get me a bottle of Cyrus Noble whiskey? I'm kind of stuck here right now."

"Well, sure," said Debs. "I can do that."

"I want to give old Fuller a drink," said Bond. "Hell, it's his wedding day."

"I'll get it and be right back here," said Debs.

"Thanks, Oogene."

He watched while Debs hurried on over to the Rattlesnake and went inside. It was only a couple of minutes before the stableman re-emerged from the saloon with a bottle in his hand, and in another minute he had handed the bottle to Bond and gone on his way. Bond went inside the office, grabbed two cups, and headed down the hallway to the last cell.

"Here," he said, handing the bottle through the bars to Fuller. "Open this up."

"What's this?" said Fuller.

"What the hell does it look like?"

"I know what it is. I mean, what is it doing back here, or to be more precise, what are you doing with it back here?"

He got the lid off the bottle and held it back out toward Bond. Bond did not take it. Instead he held a cup out for Fuller to pour whiskey into. Fuller poured it about half full, and Bond held out the other cup. When Fuller had poured a drink into the second cup, Bond handed one cup through the bars.

"A wedding calls for a toast or something, don't it?" said Bond. "Well, here's to your wedding."

He took a good long drink, and Fuller did the same.

"It just don't seem right," said Bond. "A man gets married, and then his new wife goes off and he goes right back in the jail cell."

Fuller recalled the erotic episode which had led to his wedding, and he took another drink.

"No," he said, "it does not seem right at all."

While Bond and Fuller were getting drunk in the jail, Ellie and Lottie were becoming friends over lunch at Bubba's Cafe.

"It was a nice wedding," said Lottie. "The whole town was there, just about."

"I don't think it would have pleased my mother," said Ellie.

"No, I guess not. You coming from rich folks and all. What'll you do if they don't let your man out of jail?"

"I hadn't really thought of that," said Ellie. "I don't believe that he's guilty."

90

"Honey," said Lottie, "he wouldn't be the first innocent man to hang."

"No, I suppose not," said Ellie, and she became quiet and thoughtful. "I suppose I must consider that possibility."

"Always plan for the worst," said Lottie. "Then if it don't happen, you'll have a pleasant surprise. If it does, you'll be prepared."

"Yes. I guess so."

"So?"

"So what?"

"So what'll you do if they find him guilty?"

"I—I don't know," said Ellie.

"Well then, I'll tell you," said Lottie. "You'll turn right around and go back home to that big ranch and those rich parents of yours. They'll look down their noses at you for awhile, but they'll take you back in. And most important, they'll raise that baby for you. You're going to need them, Ellie. Believe me. You don't want to wind up—."

"Wind up what?" said Ellie.

"Like me."

Lottie reached for her coffee cup out of nervousness and found it empty.

"Hey, Bubba," she shouted. "What's a girl have to do around here to get a refill?"

There were some snickers around the room. A couple of women at a far table looked down their noses. But Bubba brought a coffee pot and refilled the two cups.

"All you got to do is holler, sugar," he said, "and old Bubba comes a-running."

"Thank you," said Ellie.

Bubba took his coffee pot and left, and Ellie looked at Lottie.

"Are you—are you very unhappy?" she said.

"What? Hell, no. I'm doing just fine. Don't get me wrong. Anyhow, I've had my chances. I could get married right now if I wanted to. Denver keeps begging me to, but I won't do it."

"You don't love him?" asked Ellie.

"It ain't that," said Lottie. "Love? That's no way to plan a life. Did you get married because of love?"

"Well, no, but—."

"You see? Well, I won't either. Denver's a good man. He keeps telling me that it don't matter to him what I am. He says if I quit and marry him, it'll all be forgot, and from then on, it'll be just me and him. But if a man marries a whore, how can he ever forget it?"

"Maybe he can't," said Ellie, "but if he loves her enough, maybe it won't matter."

"I almost gave in to him the last time," said Lottie, "but I couldn't. I couldn't let myself do it. I couldn't be sure that I wasn't just doing it because I'm so scared lately."

"What are you afraid of?" said Ellie.

"You ain't heard about the killings?"

"Just the murder of that man Coker Jack that they're holding Richard for. That's all. Have there been others?"

"Oh, God," said Lottie. "Let's pay up and get out of here and go someplace real private where we can talk. I've got a lot to tell you."

Ben Kane opened the door to his son's bedroom. Just as he expected, Donald was still asleep. He walked over to the side of the bed and stared down at the lump under the covers for a long moment. At last, he reached down and patted the lump on the shoulder. There was no response. He shook the form a bit, and it moved.

"Donald," he said.

Donald rolled over under the covers and groaned.

"Donald, get up."

Donald's head came out from under the covers. He squinted his eyes up at his father. Then he pulled the comforter back up over his head.

"Leave me alone," he groaned.

"Donald, it's way past noon. What do you want to sleep the whole day away for? Get up and get dressed."

"Why should I? God damn, let me sleep, will you?"

Kane suddenly ripped the covers off. He grabbed Donald by the arm and pulled him up to a sitting position.

"I won't have you talking like that in my house," he said. "What's happened to you? Where did I go wrong with you, boy? What do you think you're going to do with your life? You're going to wake up one of these fine days and find me dead and gone. What'll you do then? Who'll you live off of then?"

"Oh, I expect I'll find someone," said Donald. "Even if I don't, what will it matter? If you're dead and gone, it won't be your worry anyway."

"Well, it's my worry now."

"Yeah, well, just let it go," said Donald.

"I want you to get out and get a job. If you don't want to get a job then go back to school."

"You'd like for me to go back to Austin,

93

wouldn't you?" said Donald. "That would get me out of your hair."

"That's not the reason," said Kane. "You were almost through. Three and a half years, and you just quit. No reason. You just quit. All that time and all that money wasted. And that's not the worst of it. The rest of your life will be wasted. Go back and finish. I'll still pay your way. You've got to do something with your life."

Donald stood up and walked over to a table on the other side of the room where he found a ready roll cigarette and a match. He struck the match and lit the cigarette.

"Smoking, drinking, gambling, whoring. I don't know what's next," said Kane.

"Maybe I'll take up bank robbery," said Donald. "Then you could organize a posse and chase me down."

"Donald, — ."

"Hey, old man. You came in here to wake me up, didn't you? Well, look. I'm up and awake. All right? If you'll get out of here, I'll get dressed."

Kane turned and stalked out of the room and on out of the house. He kept walking until he was back at his office. He went in and looked around. Bond was not there, but the door to the cells was standing open. He must be back there for some reason. Kane walked over to the open door.

"Denver," he called out. "You back there?"

"Yes, sir," said Denver. "I'm right back here watching the prisoner."

Kane heard a laugh. He didn't think that it was Bond. It must have been Fuller. He shrugged it off and went over to his desk to sit down. He would be glad when the judge showed up and he could get rid of Fuller one way or another. He had plenty of other problems to worry about. He heard more laughter from down the hallway, and he got up and walked to the door again.

"Denver," he called. "What's going on down there?"

"Nothing much, Sheriff. Everything's fine. Just fine."

Kane started down the hallway.

"He's coming," said Fuller.

"Hide that bottle," said Bond.

Kane stepped up to Bond. He could smell the whiskey. He looked at Fuller in the cell, and he could see that Fuller was drunk. He didn't need to see the bottle to know what had been going on.

"I never thought I'd see you drunk on the job," he said to Bond.

"Well, sir," said Bond, his speech slightly slurred, "I didn't either, by God. But this here was poor old Fuller's wedding day, and it just didn't seem right that we just put him right back in the cell right after he got hitched."

Bond looked like he was about to start blubbering, and Kane recalled that Lottie Kuntz had given her ring to Fuller to use in the ceremony. Bond's feelings for Lottie were no secret, and Kane suspected that Bond was thinking about more than just Fuller's dilemma. He turned without a word and walked back down the hallway and out into the office. He got the keys from his desk and went back to the cell.

"Take off your gunbelt," he said to Bond.

Bond fumbled with his gunbelt and managed to get it off. Kane took it and slung it over his shoulder. Then he unlocked the cell door.

"Get in there, Denver," he said. "You might as well finish off that bottle with him and then sleep it off. I'll let you out when you sober up."

Bond went into the cell, and Kane shut and locked the door. He went back down the hallway, and Fuller and Bond saw the big door at the end of the hall shut. They heard the sound of Kane locking it from the other side. Fuller brought the bottle out from behind his back.

"I bet you need another drink," he said.

Bond held out his cup.

"Yes, I do," he said. "I surely damn do."

Chapter Ten

"The first one was Bridgit," said Lottie. "Bridgit. She was a sweet young thing. She should never have been in this business. Not her. Of course, there's some would say none of us should be in it. That's what Gospel Bill says. But I think we serve a purpose. I'm not ashamed of what I do for a living. It's honest. I never cheat. And I don't steal. I give pleasure. What could be wrong with that?"

They were standing in front of a wooden cross in Jubilation's Boot Hill. Lottie took a long pause.

"Yeah," she said finally, "Bridgit was the first one. She just didn't come out of her room one day, and we finally went to see if there was anything wrong. There was. She was lying in her bed. She was naked, and she'd been stabbed to death. It was awful."

Lottie turned and walked away from the cross, and Ellie followed her. The next stop was only a few feet away.

"Next was Georgia," said Lottie. "She called herself the Georgia Peach. No one knew what her right name was or if she had any family anywhere or anything else about her. But she'd been around a time or two. You could tell that about her, and even if you couldn't tell it, she'd let you know. She was proud of her experience and of how tough she was. She used to say, 'Whatever it is, I can take it. Hell, I probably already have somewhere, sometime or other.' I guess you might say that Georgia was my best friend. She was good as gold, she was. A customer went up to see her one night and found her. The same as Bridgit."

Lottie walked over to the next grave, right beside that of the Georgia Peach.

"This is Mary Magdalene," she said. "Most girls in this profession don't use their right names. She was number three. So far, the last one, but the killer ain't been caught, so who knows if Mary will be the last. I could be next. Anyone could be. Any one of us local whores, that is. We're fair game just now."

"Doesn't the sheriff have any leads?" said Ellie.

"If he does, he's keeping it to himself. As far as we know, it's a complete mystery."

"But what about the man who killed Mr. Coker Jack?" said Ellie. "If there's been a murderer loose in town for three months, isn't it possible that the same man is guilty of this latest murder?"

"Ben Kane says that it ain't the same kind of killing," said Lottie. "He says that some crazy killed the girls. Someone with a sick mind. He says that your Richard killed Coker Jack because Jack cheated him out of a bunch of money."

"Richard didn't do it," said Ellie. "I know that much. And that means that the sheriff should still be looking, and if he knows that a killer has been in this town for three months, he ought to be concentrating on finding him."

"Well," said Lottie, "nobody can tell Ben Kane

how to do his job. He's always right, if you ask him. Well, let's go. Come on, honey."

Lottie started walking, but Ellie just stood for a moment as if lost in deep thought. She allowed Lottie to get several steps away, toward the edge of Boot Hill before she spoke.

"Lottie," she said.

Lottie stopped and turned, realizing for the first time that Ellie had not been following along.

"What?" she said.

"I've just decided."

"Decided what, honey?"

"I've got to get Richard out of jail."

"You mean break him out?" said Lottie. "Honey, that's crazy. You can't do that."

"If I have to, as a last resort, I'll do that, but that's not what I meant."

"What then?"

"I've got to find out who the real killer is and prove that Richard is innocent. That's all."

The bottle was empty. Denver Bond was sitting in a corner of the cell on the floor leaning against the wall. He was asleep—or passed out. Richard Fuller was sitting up on the cot. He was drunk. He felt woozy. His head was reeling, and he was thinking deep thoughts. I'm a married man, he said to himself. Ellie is Mrs. Fuller. Lovely Ellie. And here I sit. I'm going to be a daddy, too. Daddy. To a little baby. My baby and Ellie's. Little boy. Or little girl. If they hang me, I'll never see it. Never know. Never know its name. My baby. Who the hell killed Coker Jack anyway? I didn't do it. Why does Kane want to pin it on me? I didn't do anything to Kane. Damn him anyway. Damn it all. I've got to get out of here.

He stood up and found his legs wobbly, and his head started to spin unmercifully. He sat heavily back down on the cot and fell backwards, bumping his head against the wall.

"Ouch," he said out loud. "Damn it all to bloody hell."

He turned and lay back and for a few painful moments, the cell seemed to spin round and round. Then he fell asleep. And then he dreamed. He was in a field with Ellie, and they were making love. It was beautiful. Ellie's body was beautiful. And Richard was happy, perfectly happy. He could tell that she, too, was happy, and the world was a perfect place to be. But the scene changed on Richard, and he was sitting at a table with Coker Jack across from him, and Coker Jack kept laying aces on the table and kept sweeping up Richard's money. The money in front of Coker Jack kept getting piled higher and higher, and finally Richard sprang up from his seat and overturned the table, flinging cards and chips and money all over the place. Coker Jack was up on his feet with a gun in each hand, cursing and shooting. Bullets whizzed by Richard's ears, and Richard couldn't seem to find his gun to defend himself. Then he saw a bullet in mid-flight. It was coming directly at him, at his heart, and he watched in horror, but he couldn't move out of its path, and then the scene changed. He saw Ellie again, but she was different. She was standing alone in the field, the same field in which they had made love. But she was all alone. The wind was blowing and the prairie grasses looked like waves in the ocean, and Ellie was very much alone, but her belly was greatly swollen. And then there was a child walking along beside a road.

It was just barely old enough to walk, and Richard was walking beside it. It was a beautiful little child, and it was his own. He knew that. He reached out his hand to take the tiny hand of the child which was reaching up toward him, but just as he was about to touch the hand, everything went black, and out of the blackness, the grotesque image of the twisted and mangled body of Coker Jack emerged. It was battered almost beyond recognition, and it was covered with blood and it was lying in a vast pool of blood. And then he woke up.

He was lying on the cot in the jail cell, and he was sweating profusely. He was staring at the ceiling, and his head was throbbing. He rolled his head slowly to one side, and he saw Denver Bond still unconscious there in the corner of the cell. And he wondered what painful images might be running through the deputy's head. Strange, he thought, how one can look so peaceful on the outside. Strange.

Lottie had taken Ellie to the Rattlesnake and upstairs to her room. She had found all the other working girls but one. That one, known as Skeeter, was occupied with a customer.

"Who's she with?" Lottie had asked.

"Some new guy in town," said Bonnie Bedamn. "Nobody knows him."

"Who's your friend?" said Lola Brand. "And what's this all about?"

"You got a new girl, Lottie?" said Queenie.

"Just shut up and show some manners," said Lottie. "No, I ain't got a new girl here. This is a friend. This is Mrs. Richard Fuller, as if you didn't know it already. You were all at the wedding, weren't you?"

"Yeah," said Queenie, "but they're going to hang him, and she's got to do something for a living, ain't she?"

"They're not going to hang him," said Ellie.

"Oh, well," said Queenie, "excuse my ass. I guess you're just not going to let them do it."

"That's right," said Ellie. "I'm not."

"All right, all right," said Lottie. "Just keep your pants on. All of you. Mrs. Fuller—."

"Please call me Ellie."

"Ellie, here, wanted to meet all of you. She wants to ask some questions."

"What about?" said Bonnie Bedamn.

"If you'll all just keep quiet for a few minutes, I'll let her talk. Then you'll find out. Ellie, we're all here except Skeeter. She's—occupied. This is Bonnie, Lola and Queenie. That's all of us that's left here. Five of us. You saw where the others are now."

"Yes," said Ellie. "Well, I'll get right to the point. I don't believe that—my husband is guilty of murder. And I don't intend to just sit by and watch them condemn him for something he didn't do. The sheriff seems to have decided that the case is closed. I think it calls for further investigation, and that means that I'm going to have to do it myself."

"You're going to investigate a murder?" said Queenie.

"Of course," said Ellie. "If I don't, who will?"

"Why not?" said Bonnie Bedamn. "Why, I bet she could do as good a job of it as Ben Kane."

"Yeah," said Lola. "Even if Ben wanted to do it. Men ain't so smart. No smarter than we are."

"If we're so smart," said Queenie, "why are we a bunch of whores?"

"Because the men won't let us be anything else,"

102

said Bonnie. "Wives or whores. That's all they think we're good for."

"All right," said Queenie, "so she's going to look for Coker Jack's killer. So she might find out who really did it. So what's all that got to do with us?"

"Maybe nothing," said Ellie, "but let me tell you what I'm thinking. From what I've been able to find out so far, when Coker Jack's body was discovered, Sheriff Kane immediately suspected Richard. Richard had lost money in a poker game with Coker Jack, and Richard had accused him of cheating. Coker Jack went for his guns, but Richard pulled his first. There was no shooting, but the sheriff figured that Richard had motive for killing Coker Jack based on that little episode."

"I saw all that," said Bonnie. "That's how it happened all right. But if your Richard had wanted to kill Jack, he could have done it right then and there. Everyone would have sworn that it was self-defense. Why would he wait until dark and bash the man's brains out?"

"Exactly," said Ellie. "But when Richard became convinced that he was the sheriff's number one suspect, he decided to leave town. That's when he was arrested, and Sheriff Kane says that proves that Richard was guilty. He was trying to run away."

"There's more than one reason to run away," said Lola. "Sure, a guilty man will run, but so will an innocent man if he can see that he's being set up for a frame."

"I agree," said Ellie, "and I believe Richard. He told me that he didn't do it. So I'm working from the belief that the sheriff has arrested the wrong man. That means the guilty man is still out there somewhere."

"Right," said Bonnie.

"So where do you start looking? It seems to me that there are two trails to follow in this case. One is the one the sheriff followed, but he didn't stay with it long enough. Who had a reason to kill Coker Jack? If Coker Jack was cheating and winning, then anyone in that card game who lost money could be a suspect. And that probably wasn't the first game in which he had cheated people out of their money. There could also be other reasons that people around here might want to kill the man."

"What's the other trail?" said Queenie.

"There have been other murders here," said Ellie. "Friends of yours. Three of them in three months, I understand. If there's already a killer in this town, it seems to me that whoever that killer is, he must be considered a suspect in this killing too."

"But it ain't the same kind of killing," said Queenie."

"I realize that," said Ellie, "and that's what Sheriff Kane says, too. But I still think that it ought to be considered."

"Yeah," said Bonnie. "Me too. Anyone that would do what he done to Mary and Georgia and Bridgit would do anything. He's got to be crazy, and a crazy man will do anything."

Queenie stood up and paced the floor nervously. Then she turned on Ellie.

"All right," she said. "So your hubbie didn't kill Coker Jack, and Ben Kane ain't looking for who did. Maybe the same creep that killed the girls is the guilty party. So what does all that have to do with us? I mean, what do we do?"

"First of all," said Ellie, "just think about it. Remember anything you can about who was with those three girls and who might have had it in for Coker Jack. Have you had any particularly strange acting — customers? Anything you can think of that might help."

"Honey," said Lottie, "all men are strange acting when they come to us. You just don't know."

"But if we all put our minds to it," said Ellie, "maybe we'll come up with something. Even if you don't think of something from before, keep your minds open to whatever happens from here on. If you see or hear anything that will help, anything that you think might help, tell each other, and tell me."

"All right," said Queenie.

"Above all," said Ellie, "we all know who the man's favorite victims are, so be careful. Whatever you do, be careful."

The meeting broke up, and Ellie was on her way out. She stepped into the hallway from Lottie's room, and a door just across the way opened. Franklin Smith stepped out. He saw Ellie, and his face turned a deep red. He ducked his head, and hurried on down the hall. Lottie was standing in her own doorway as a young woman appeared in the doorway that Smith had come out of.

"Wait up, Ellie," said Lottie.

Ellie turned back to face Lottie, but Lottie was looking across the hall.

"Come here," she said to the girl in the other doorway. "I want you to meet someone. This is my friend, Ellie, Mrs. Richard Fuller."

"Yeah," said the other. "I seen the wedding."

"Ellie, this is Skeeter."

Chapter Eleven

Lottie gave Skeeter a quick and short summary of the meeting she had just missed.

"I'll tell her more about it," she said to Ellie. "You don't have to hang around if you don't want to."

"There's not really much more to tell," said Ellie. "I think you summed it up nicely."

"It's funny though," said Skeeter. "That guy that just left?"

"What about him?" said Lottie.

"Mr. Franklin Smith," said Ellie. "He came to town on the same stage as I did."

"It's funny," said Skeeter. "He was asking about them, too."

"About who?" said Lottie.

"Bridgit and them. That's all he done. I mean, he didn't do nothing. He paid me, but all he wanted was to ask questions about them."

* * *

Franklin Smith asked his questions elsewhere, too, and soon just about everyone in Jubilation knew that the big stranger who had come on the stage was asking questions about the murdered women. The following morning, Smith was in the Rattlesnake as soon as it opened for business. He went straight to the bar.

"What can I do for you?" said the bartender.

"You got coffee?" said Smith.

"Sure."

The bartender poured a cup of coffee and put it on the bar in front of Smith. Smith dug into his pocket and paid the man. He took a sip of the hot, black liquid.

"Ah," he said. "That's a good cup of coffee. My first this morning, too. Real good."

"Glad you like it," said the bartender.

"My name's Smith. Franklin Smith. I'm new here."

"Yeah," said the bartender. "I know. This is a small town. Word gets around."

Smith chuckled.

"I guess so," he said. "What can I call you?"

"Arch."

"Well, Arch," said Smith, "what else have you heard about me?"

"They say you came in on the stage the other night along with that woman who married Fuller down at the jailhouse."

"That I did. That I did. What else?"

"They say you've been asking questions around town about them girls that was killed here."

"Yes," said Smith. "I have been."

"I wondered when you'd get around to me."

"Have you got anything to tell me?"

"I guess that depends on what you already know," said Arch.

"Not much. I know that the first girl killed was called Bridgit. I haven't heard a last name."

"She never used one," said "Arch. "Nobody can answer that question around here. Now that she's dead and buried, I guess no one anywhere will ever know."

"The second was known as the Georgia Peach."

"Right," said Arch. "Same story. I don't even know if Georgia was her name. That's what we called her."

"And Mary Magdalene?" said Smith.

"I doubt if that was her real name," said Arch. "Don't you?"

"Nobody knows the real names of any of them?" said Smith.

"Mr. Smith, girls in that profession don't often go by their right names. They don't want to shame their families, if they have any. You know?"

"I suppose so," said Smith. "They were all found the same way? Naked in their beds? Throats cut?"

"Yeah."

"No clues?"

"None at all."

"Did they have anything in common? I mean, other than their profession and their workplace?"

"Not that I know of," said Arch. "Let me ask you a question, Mr. Smith."

"Shoot," said Smith.

"What's your interest in this?"

"Idle curiosity, Arch," said Smith. "Nothing more, nothing less."

"Yeah?" said Arch. "Well, I know nothing more.

Okay?"

"Sure. Thanks for the coffee."

Smith shoved the cup toward Arch and headed for the door. He was just about to reach it, when Ben Kane stepped in and stood deliberately in front of him.

"Smith?" said Kane.

"Yeah. I'm Frank Smith. What do you want with me, Sheriff?"

"I understand that you've been all over town asking about the killing of those whores. What's it all about?"

"I just got here, Sheriff," said Smith. "That was the first thing I heard about. I'm just naturally curious, I guess. Anything wrong with that?"

"Maybe. I've got a crazy killer on my hands. Then a stranger comes to town who seems overly interested in the killings. That makes me just a little suspicious, or you might say, naturally curious."

"Like you said, Sheriff, I'm a stranger here. I got no interest. I'm just nosey."

"That could get you in trouble," said Kane.

"Is that a threat, Sheriff?"

"Just good advice, Mr. Smith. By the way, what's your business in town?"

"No business, Sheriff. I'm just passing through."

"Take my advice. Pass on. Go on wherever it is you're headed."

Smith put his hands on his hips and cocked his head. He looked Kane in the eyes.

"Sheriff," he said, "I've got money in my pockets. I'm no vagrant. I haven't broken any laws, and I won't be bullied or harassed. There's no law against asking questions."

"Don't say I didn't warn you," said Kane, and he

turned and walked out of the saloon. Smith stood there for a moment, looked over his shoulder at Arch and shrugged. Then he too walked out.

Kane went back to his office and got the keys out of his desk. He unlocked the big door and walked down the hallway to the cell where Bond and Fuller were locked up drunk.

"Denver," he said, "are you sober?"

Bond stood up from where he had been sitting on the floor. He kept his head down though.

"Yes, sir," he said. "I am, but I've got an awful headache."

Kane unlocked the cell door.

"Come on out," he said.

"Hey, Denver," said Fuller.

Bond looked back at Fuller.

"Thanks."

"Sure," said Bond. He walked on out into the hallway, and Kane shut and locked the cell door. "I'll see you at lunch time," said Bond, and he and Kane went on down the hallway and back out into the office. Kane shut and locked the big door.

"Denver," he said, "go get yourself some breakfast. Drink lots of coffee. Then get back here ready to work."

"Yes, sir," said Bond, and he left the office and headed straight for the nearest cafe. It was Bubba's. He stepped inside and looked around. The tables were all occupied, but at one table, Ellie Fuller sat alone. She was drinking coffee. Bond walked over to the table and took off his hat.

"Mrs. Fuller," he said.

"Oh, good morning, Deputy," said Ellie.

110

"Can I join you?"

"Please do."

Bond pulled out a chair and sat down.

"I'm feeling a little groggy," he said. "I just spent the night in jail with your husband and a bottle."

"You got drunk?" said Ellie.

"Yeah," said Bond. "I'm afraid so."

"Both of you?"

"Yes, ma'am."

"How is Richard this morning?"

"Aw, he's all right. Probably not as bad off as me."

"Well," said Ellie, "it was probably good for both of you, as long as you don't make a habit of it. I've known my father to do that on occasion. It's a great relaxer, I imagine."

"Yes, ma'am," said Bond.

"Please, call me Ellie."

"All right. If you'll call me Denver."

"Agreed," said Ellie.

"I've been wishing that I could get a chance to talk to you," said Bond. "I feel kind of bad about Richard. Me being a deputy and all."

"Don't feel bad," said Ellie. "As long as Richard is in jail, I'm glad that you're there."

Bubba walked up to the table just then with a pad in his hand. Ellie had already ordered her breakfast, so Bond ordered his and coffee. Bubba ambled away.

"I don't believe he's guilty," said Ellie. She felt a little strange and even foolish for having blurted it out so suddenly. She thought that perhaps she should have led up to it in a less abrupt way. But she had felt a need to confide in this man, this deputy sheriff, this employee of Ben Kane and lover of her new friend, Lottie.

Bubba came back with Bond's coffee and with a pot from which he refilled Ellie's cup. Then he ambled away again. Bond took a sip of the hot coffee and winced. His head was still throbbing. He set the cup down and stared into it.

"Me neither," he said. "But I don't know what to do about it. Ben, he's got his mind set. He won't listen to nothing different."

"Denver," said Ellie, lowering her voice, "I'm conducting my own investigation."

"What?"

"I intend to find out who the real killer is. I can't take a chance with the trial. If the sheriff won't keep this investigation open, then I have to do it myself. That's all there is to it."

"My God, Ellie," said Bond. "You be careful. That could be dangerous."

"We're talking about the life of my husband," said Ellie.

"Well, look. I can't help you out any. I mean, not officially, but if you need anything, if there's anything I can do for you, like on the sly, you be sure and let me know."

"I will," said Ellie. "Thank you."

"And I'll kind of keep my eyes and ears open, you know. I'll do what I can. You know, I like old Richard. And I know that you've made friends with Lottie. I appreciate that. Most of them, you know, decent folks around here won't have anything to do with her. I owe you for that."

"I think I know how you feel about Lottie," said Ellie, "and from what I've seen of her, I think she's a fine woman. I like her a lot."

"I want to marry her," said Bond.

"I know," said Ellie, "and I'll do what I can to help you out with that."

Just then Bubba came back to their table with the breakfasts, and they stopped talking. After they had been left alone again, they each ate a few bites in silence. Then Ellie spoke again.

"I want to see Richard," she said.

"After we finish up here," said Bond, "give me a few minutes. I'll go back to the office, and then I imagine Ben will take off and leave it with me. Why don't you come on over after he's gone. I'll let you in."

Ellie watched through the front window of the cafe after Bond left. She could see the sheriff's office, and she saw Bond go inside. A few minutes later, she saw Kane leave. She got up and paid her bill and left the cafe. She walked briskly over to the sheriff's office and went inside. Bond got the keys and opened the big door.

"Hey, old buddy," he hollered down the hallway. "You've got yourself a visitor."

He stepped aside to allow Ellie room to walk through the door. Fuller was up on his feet, looking down the hallway. It didn't take him long to recognize his visitor, and even though she walked, as usual, briskly, it seemed to him that it took a long time for her to get to his cell.

"Hello, Richard," she said. "Are they treating you well?"

"As well as can be expected," he said. "How are you?"

"I'm managing all right. Do you get enough to eat?"

113

"Oh, yeah. That's no problem."

"I could have something sent in if you're not getting enough."

"No. No," he said. "Don't bother. Really, I'm doing fine. It's just—awful boring in here. That's all. I'm—I'm glad you came."

"I had them change my registration at the hotel," she said. "I registered originally as Ellie McKee. I had them change it to Mrs. Richard Fuller."

Fuller chuckled.

"I guess that will take some getting used to," he said. "Ellie, don't you think that you should go back home?"

"No, Richard. I did think about it, but I decided otherwise. You're my husband, and I'm not going to leave you here."

"But what if they find me guilty?" he said. "You don't want to be around for the—."

"That's not going to happen," she snapped, interrupting him.

"It could happen," he said. "You have to be prepared for the worst."

"Funny," said Ellie. "That's what Lottie said."

"Lottie?" said Fuller.

"Yes. We had lunch together after the wedding."

"Oh," said Fuller. "Well, she was right. It wouldn't be the first time an innocent man was convicted. You hear about that sort of thing happening, and it makes you wonder how often it happens that we don't hear about."

"I'm not just sitting back and depending on the justice system to work, Richard," said Ellie. "I know you're innocent, and I know that Sheriff Kane has quit investigating, so I'm looking into it myself."

"Looking into what?" said Fuller.

"I intend to find out who the real murderer is and prove it," she said. "That's the only way I know of to ensure your release."

"Ellie," Fuller protested.

"I have help," she said. "I don't want you to be worried about my safety. We're going to be very careful, but we're determined to see this through."

"Who is we?"

"Lottie and her—business associates," said Ellie. "And the deputy sheriff, Mr. Bond. Denver. Your friend. But you have to keep that quiet. He doesn't want the sheriff to know."

"Oh, God," said Fuller. "I don't know what to say. Damn it, I wish I could get out of here."

"You will," she said. "For now, just tell me, if you can, who besides yourself could be said to have had a motive for killing Coker Jack."

Chapter Twelve

J.W. McKee was not a tall man, but he was stockily built and tough as a keg of nails. Probably every bone in his body had been broken at one time or another over the years, but the healing process had only served to crust him over and make his leathery old hide that much harder. He walked with the perpetual, rolling limp of an old cowboy, hunkered over, partly out of habit, partly from pain. His face had a rough and mean look about it, and his fists were hard and large for the rest of his size. In spite of his age, his black hair was mostly still black, and his fading gray eyes still had a twinkle about them. J.W. was known as a hard man and a tough man, a man occasionally even mean. He was a man who had worked hard and fought hard to get what he wanted out of life, and he was a man who usually did get what he wanted. To the ranch hands who worked for him, he was king. To the nearby town, he was the local economy. Therefore, when J.W. was upset, everyone was upset.

And J.W. was upset. He and his wife Mollie had gotten up one morning to discover that their daughter Ellie, the light of their collective lives, was gone. There were a few items of clothing missing, and her own horse and saddle were gone too. Though it was difficult for J.W. and Mollie to believe, it appeared as if she had run away from home.

"It's that God damned gambler," J.W. had said.

He couldn't imagine anything else that would have caused Ellie to leave of her own accord. Ellie had been a perfect daughter for nineteen years. Oh, she was headstrong. She had always been like that. She liked having her own way, and she usually got it, too, but J.W. had always liked that about her. She was a lot like him. Underneath that pretty, soft-looking exterior, she was tough. Just like her old man. She had grown up on the range, running with the cowboys. She was an only child, and someday the whole ranch would be hers, and J.W. knew that she would be able to handle it. He had seen to that, and that had always been a source of special pride to J.W. But then she had a polish over it all that J.W. never had, never could have. That had come from Mollie. Mollie had always liked parlor music and the latest good books and proper and up-to-date female fashions. And she had passed all that along to Ellie. Ellie had absorbed just about everything from both her parents, as different as they were, and therefore, yes, she had been perfect. They had never, even had harsh words. Not really. Not until that gambler had come along. He had been the cause of their first real argument, and after he had left the territory, Ellie had acted different somehow. She seemed to have lost her accustomed gaiety, her carefree approach to life in general. J.W. decided that the gambler probably hadn't left at all, not until the night that he sneaked back onto the ranch and spirited Ellie away. J.W. had taken out a long bullwhip and attached it to his saddle. It would go everywhere with him from now on.

"When I find that son of a bitch," he had said, "I'm

117

going to peel all the hide off his back."

And then he had sent the boys out, the cowpunchers. He had sent them out in all directions in search of Ellie and the gambler.

"Find them both and bring them back," he had said.

"How do you want that gambler brought back, boss?" a cowboy had asked.

"Alive," said J.W.

"Mr. McKee," another had boldly asked, "what if Miss Ellie don't want to come along?"

It was a good question. No one who knew J.W. McKee could imagine laying hands on his daughter.

"Bring her back," J.W. had said, and they had seen his jaws tighten with the words.

So the cowboys had ridden out in all directions, and J.W. had ridden too. He had never been one to leave the work to others, no matter what the task.

It had been a long day, and J.W. had just unsaddled his horse and turned it loose in the corral. He had gone into the house where Mollie had greeted him with a questioning, pleading look. In answer, he just shook his heavy head and walked over to the liquor cabinet to pour himself a whiskey.

"Supper's almost ready," Mollie said, and J.W. winced at the sadness in her voice. Mollie headed back toward the kitchen, and he took note of how slowly she moved. He tossed down the shot of whiskey he had poured himself, then poured another and moved across the room to his favorite chair where he sat down heavily with a groan. Then there was a knock at the door.

"Who is it?" he called out.

"Sandy," came the answer.

"Come on in," said J.W. "It ain't locked."

A cowboy, perhaps thirty years old, let himself in and stepped a few feet into the room. He held his hat in his hands so that it covered up his belly. Sandy MacColl was J.W.'s foreman. He had been with J.W. for fifteen years, and J.W. trusted Sandy completely. In J.W.'s absence, Sandy MacColl had complete authority on the ranch, and everyone knew that. Next to J.W., he was probably the most feared and respected man in the territory.

"I just come back from town, boss," said Sandy. "I rode in first thing this morning."

J.W. knew that already, of course. He had known where every hand on the ranch was headed that morning. He waited for the rest of whatever it might be that Sandy had to tell him. Just then Mollie stepped into the doorway from the kitchen. She had heard the noise accompanying Sandy's entrance, and she stood there expectantly.

"I found Samson," said Sandy.

Mollie's mouth opened slightly, and she took a step forward. J.W. came up out of his chair.

"Where?" he demanded.

"Old man Talley had him," said Sandy. "He had him back in a stall. He said Ellie come in a-wanting to sell him. He bought him, but he was afraid to put him up for sale. I told him you'd probably buy him back."

"Was that gambler with her?" said J.W.

"No, sir. Talley said she was by herself."

"Why did she sell Sampson?" said Mollie.

"Well, ma'am," said Sandy, "there's more. I'm just trying to find the right way to tell it all."

"Just spit it out, damn it," said J.W.

"Yes, sir. After I found Sampson, I went all over town asking questions. I found out that Ellie had bought herself a railroad passage down into Texas.

119

Claybourn at the station sold it to her. He said she didn't seem to have no proper destination in mind. She just asked him how far south into Texas the railroad would take her, and then she bought a ticket that far."

"One ticket?" said J.W.

"Yes, sir."

"Damn," said J.W.

"There's one other thing," said Sandy.

"What?" said J.W.

"This here letter come for you. For both of you."

He reached a hand out from behind his hat and held the letter toward J.W. Mollie rushed over to stand beside her husband as he snatched the letter from Sandy's hand.

"It was mailed from Texas. Must have come back on the return train." said Sandy.

"It's Ellie's writing," said Mollie.

J.W. ripped open the envelope and fumbled with his thick fingers to unfold the letter. His hands shook so that the letter rattled as he read it. Then Mollie took it from his hands. She had already read it, but she read it again. Neither parent spoke for another minute. Sandy stood, hat in hands, waiting for further orders or for dismissal. Finally Mollie looked into J.W.'s eyes.

"Oh, God," she said.

She put her hands on his shoulders and leaned a cheek against his chest. J.W. put his arms around her and held her tight. He looked over her shoulder toward Sandy.

"Call off the search," he said. "Put the boys back to work. Tell Orville he'll be in charge here for awhile. First thing in the morning, have two horses ready for me and you.

"Yes, sir," said Sandy. He hesitated a moment

thinking that J.W. would say something more, but the old man had finished. "Uh, excuse me, boss," he said. "Where we going?"

"We're going after Ellie," said J.W. "Where else?"

"Yes, sir," said Sandy. "Is that all?"

"Till morning," said J.W.

"Good night, Sandy," said Mollie, turning to face him, "and thank you."

"Yes, ma'am," said Sandy. "Good night."

The cowboy let himself out, leaving the worried parents to themselves.

"You were right about the telephone," said J.W.

"What?"

"You wanted me to have a telephone installed with a line into town. I said no. Didn't want the damn new-fangled contraption in my house. Well, you were right, as usual. If we had a telephone, we'd have figured this all out sooner. So go ahead. Have it put in."

"All right," said Mollie. "If you say so. J.W., what are you going to do?"

"I'm going to bring them back," he said.

"Them?"

"She went after a husband," said J.W. "A father for our grandbaby. She'll have him. I'll see to that."

Mollie looked at J.W. in time to see a large tear roll down one wrinkled old cheek. She knew that he would not want her to see that, so she turned quickly away.

"I'll see to supper," she said, and for the first time since the disappearance of Ellie, she felt that everything was going to turn out all right.

The sun was not yet up the following morning when Sandy brought the two saddled horses to the front porch of the ranch house. His own extra clothing was packed into a saddle roll and tied on behind his saddle. He had just walked up to the porch when the front door opened and J.W. stepped out. Mollie was right behind him. J.W. gave his wife a kiss.

"Bring them home," said Mollie.

"I will, Mollie. I promise you."

"And you be careful. I want you back too, safely. Be careful."

J.W. stepped down off the porch and tied his own saddle roll onto the other horse. Then he climbed into the saddle.

"Let's go," he said.

The ride into town took almost until noon, and J.W. and Sandy tied up in front of the railroad depot. J.W. stalked into the station. Claybourn was there behind the cage.

"Claybourn, you son of a bitch," said J.W., "I want two tickets to the same damn place my daughter went."

"Yes, sir," said Claybourn, trembling a little. "That'd be the end of the line down in Texas."

"Wherever," said J.W. "And I want to take along three horses and saddles."

"Yes, sir."

J.W. walked to the big rail map which was hanging on the wall and studied it for a moment.

"What do you mean end of the line?" he said. "The damn tracks run all around Texas."

"Yes, sir," said Claybourn, "but you see that big area there — most of west Texas — that's just kind of circled around by the tracks?"

"Yeah," said J.W.

"And you see that little piece of track that just runs a ways into the circle and then quits?"

J.W. nodded and growled, a kind of affirmative growl.

"Well, sir, the end of that spur, that's what we call the end of track down in west Texas."

"All right," said J.W. "When does the damn train leave?"

Claybourn pulled a watch out of his pocket and checked the time.

"One o'clock," he said. "That's just a little over an hour from now."

J.W. paid Claybourn.

"Come on," he said, and he stalked back out to the hitch rail and mounted up again. Sandy followed him. J.W. led the way to Talley's stable. They found Talley inside sweeping out stalls.

"Talley," shouted J.W., "where's my horse?"

"Right down here, Mr. McKee," said Talley, and he led the way down to the far stall. J.W. was right behind him, and Sandy was right behind J.W.

"I didn't know what else to do, Mr. McKee," said Talley. "She come in here and said she wanted to sell him. I didn't know what else to do."

"How much did you pay her?" said J.W.

"I give her seventy-five dollars for the horse and thirty-five for the saddle," said Talley.

J.W. pulled out his wallet and counted out one-hundred-and-twenty-five dollars. He thrust the bills at Talley.

"There's your money back and a profit to boot," he said. "Now saddle the horse."

They got back to the railroad station and loaded the horses and saddles in plenty of time. Then they walked to the nearest bar for a drink of whiskey for the road. They got their drinks at the bar and then took them to a table and sat down. J.W. seemed to relax a little. There was nothing more he could do until time to get on the train, and then there would be nothing for him to do but sit until they reached the end of the line.

"Sandy," he said, "you know what I said before about what I was going to do to that gambler?"

"Yes, sir," said Sandy.

"Well, forget it. I want you to know this, just in case anything should happen to me along the way. I don't expect nothing to happen, but you never know. Ellie, she went down to Texas to find that man and marry up with him. If she wants him, then she's going to have him. She's — she's going to have a baby, Sandy, and that ga —. Richard Fuller is the daddy. That's what it said in that letter you brought. It was from Ellie."

Sandy took a sip of whiskey and stared down at the tabletop.

"I don't want it spread around about Ellie's condition before the wedding," said J.W., "but I thought I ought to tell you."

"Yes, sir," said Sandy.

"I mean to bring them back home, and Fuller is going to be treated with respect. He'll be my son-in-law. The father of my grandbaby. And when I die, him and Ellie will own the ranch. I'll want you to stick with them, Sandy. They'll need you."

"I'll stick, boss," said Sandy. "Hell, the ranch is the only home I ever had. I'll stick."

"God damn it," said J.W., "let's have one more. We got time, ain't we?"

"Yes, sir," said Sandy. "I believe we do have."

"Then let's have one more before we climb into that God damned smoke belching contraption. It's going to be a long God damned ride."

Chapter Thirteen

It was late night. Ellie wasn't exactly sure just how late it was, but she hadn't been able to sleep, so she had gotten out of bed and put her clothes back on. She had left the hotel and started walking down the main street of Jubilation. Most places were closed, and the lights were mostly out. Only the Rattlesnake continued to do business, its kind of business being the kind best conducted in the dark hours. Ellie was walking on the side of the street opposite the Rattlesnake, but as she passed it by, she stopped for a moment. Inside there were likely card games going on. Some men were winning money. More were probably losing. Some family man would go home broke, having bet and lost all the money he had which he should have spent on food for his family. The games might lead to fights. Someone else could be killed. Inside there were certainly men getting drunk, or drunker. Then there was the upstairs business. She thought of Bonnie and Lola and Skeeter and Queenie, but mostly she thought of her friend Lottie. She wondered if Lottie was — at work. If so, she wondered who was with her. She wondered what it was like for Lottie and the others, living like that, making a living like that. How many men? How many in a lifetime? What kinds of things did they have to do? And was it worth it? Was life worth living if one had to live like that? She liked Lottie, and she found that it was painful to think about the way in which Lottie was living, to try to imagine what Lottie might be doing at this very moment. Then she thought about Denver Bond, poor Denver. What he must be going through, to love a woman and to know. To know. She turned to resume her walk, and she almost ran into a man walking from the other direction.

"Oh," she said. "Excuse me. I should watch where I'm going."

"No, no. I'm the one who should apologize," said the man. "Allow me to introduce myself. I already know who you are. Everyone in town was at your wedding, I think. I'm Donald Kane."

"Oh," said Ellie, "you're — ."

"The sheriff's son," said Donald. "Yes. I suppose that doesn't make me very popular with you, since my father has arrested your husband for murder."

"I can't blame you for that," said Ellie. "I do think he's wrong, but I suppose he believes that he's right."

"Oh, yes. He always believes he's right. Well, if it's any comfort to you, I don't believe that your husband is a murderer either. He's a gentleman."

"You know Richard?"

"I've met him, and I've played in a card game or two with him," said Donald.

"Were you in the game the night that, well, the night that Richard and Coker Jack pulled guns on each other?" asked Ellie.

"Why, yes," said Donald. "I was."

"Who else was in that game?"

"Well, let's see," said Donald. "There was Richard Fuller and me and Coker Jack, of course. Oh, yes, there was Denver Bond, the deputy sheriff, you know."

"Yes," said Ellie, "I've met him."

"And then there was Conley. That's all. That's five, isn't it? There were five of us."

"Did everyone besides Coker Jack lose money?"

"Oh, yes. We all lost. He cheated us all. I'm sure that Richard was right about that. But of course. I see what you're getting at. Each one of us in that game is as likely to have killed Coker Jack as Richard. Right?"

"Well, yes," said Ellie. "I —."

"Oh, that's all right," said Donald. "I've thought the same thing myself. In fact, I made that suggestion to my father, but he didn't seem to be much impressed by it."

"Well, I know Deputy Bond," said Ellie, "and of course I know Richard, and now I've met you. Could you tell me anything about the other man?"

"Conley? Well, let's see. He's a farmer. He has a place way out of town. He comes in once a month. Brings the whole family, and they make a day of it. You know what I mean? I saw him climb in the wagon with his wife and kids and leave town just a little while after he left the game. Coker Jack was still alive and kicking in the Rattlesnake. I think we can forget about the old farmer."

"Well," said Ellie, "I certainly don't believe that any of the rest of you did it. Coker Jack must have had some other enemy somewhere. I'll just have to keep looking."

"Yes, well, be careful, Mrs. Fuller," said Donald.

"Murder investigation can be dangerous, I understand. By the way, don't you think that it's a little late for you to be out walking alone?"

"I'll be all right," said Ellie. "Thank you."

"Okay," said Donald, "if you're sure. I'll be on my way then. I hate to think about all the excitement going on across the street without me. See you around."

"Good night, Mr. Kane," said Ellie, and she watched as Donald crossed the street and went into the Rattlesnake. Then she resumed her walk, continuing to the end of the street. Soon she found herself back in Boot Hill, and she wondered why she had walked there. She hadn't made a conscious decision to visit the graveyard, yet she was there. She was standing in front of the grave marked "Mary Magdalene," and she could read the name on the wooden cross there under the bright light of the Texas moon. She thought about Mary and Bridgit and the Georgia Peach. And she thought about Lottie and the others back at the Rattlesnake still plying their trade. Then she heard a noise behind her, and her hand went into the handbag and came out again filled with the Webley Bulldog, and she turned toward the noise.

"Whoa. Don't shoot."

It was Franklin Smith. He was standing not six feet away with his hands in the air.

"That's the second time you've pulled that thing on me," he said. "Both times without any real need, I assure you. You may find it hard to believe, but back at, what was the name of that place? Dog Track. Yes. Dog Track. Back there at Dog Track I really was suffering from stage craziness."

"And now?" said Ellie.

"I came here looking for three graves. I think I've found them. Oh. You think that I followed you here? I didn't. I've been here for sometime. I started looking over on that side of the cemetery, and I was working my way this direction."

"These are the graves you were looking for?" asked Ellie, motioning toward the graves of the three prostitutes.

"Yes. Those are the ones."

"Why?" asked Ellie.

"Just curious, I guess," said Smith. "I've heard a lot about those murders since we arrived in town. Perhaps I'm a little bit morbid."

"That's all?"

"What else?" said Smith, raising his hands out to his sides.

"Well, then," said Ellie, "you've found them, and I'll leave you with them. Good night, Mr. Smith."

She kept the Webley in her hand as she walked a wide circle around Smith on her way out of Boot Hill. At the edge of the cemetery, she looked back again to make sure that he was still standing out there. He was, and she hurried on back into town and returned to the hotel. This time, she would sleep, she decided. If not, at least she would stay in bed.

It was almost noon by the time Bonnie Bedamn woke up. She dressed in a hurry and went across the hall to Lottie's room where she knocked on the door. There was no answer, so she hurried down the stairs and rushed over to the bar.

"Arch," she said, "have you seen Lottie this morning?"

"She went out just a little while ago," said the bartender.

"Where'd she go?"

"She didn't say."

"Damn," said Bonnie, and she hurried out into the

street. She looked up and down, then she walked quickly over to Bubba's cafe. There she found Lottie having her breakfast. Seated with Lottie was Queenie. Bonnie joined them.

"You want to order something?" asked Bubba.

"Just coffee," said Bonnie.

She fidgeted in her chair until the coffee was served. Then she took a sip. Lottie was watching her with curiosity.

"Is something wrong, Bonnie?" she said.

"No," said Bonnie. "Not exactly. There's something I got to tell you. Well, I guess I got to tell, you know, Ellie."

"What is it?" said Queenie.

"Wait a minute," said Lottie. "Not here. Let's finish up here and go over to the hotel."

They didn't find Ellie in her room at the hotel, so they went back out into the street.

"Where the hell could she be?" said Queenie.

"How should I know?" said Lottie. "She's investigating."

"What does that mean?"

"It means going around all over the place, looking at things, asking questions. She could be anyplace."

"There she is," said Bonnie, pointing toward the sheriff's office. Ellie was just coming out.

"Investigating, huh?" said Queenie. "I bet she was paying a conjugal visit to her hubby."

"Shut up," said Lottie. "Come on. Let's go meet her."

They met her on the sidewalk a couple of doors down from the jail, and after a hurried conference, they all walked back to the Rattlesnake and went upstairs to Lottie's room. Lottie shut and locked the door.

"What is it?" said Ellie

"Tell her, Bonnie," said Queenie.

"Well, I just remembered something," said Bonnie, "and I think it might be important."

"Go on," said Lottie.

"It's about Coker Jack. He was real drunk one night. It's been a couple of weeks ago, I think. Anyhow, he came up to my room, and he paid me, but then he was too drunk to do anything. You know. Anyhow, he was bragging around about what a big man he was. He told me how much money he had, and he took out a roll of bills and flashed it. He said he had all kinds of important friends, and he told me about the women he'd had, and he said that he usually didn't have to pay. He even said that some women had paid him."

"Get to the point, Bonnie," said Queenie.

"Well, then he said that he had all kinds of ways of making money. Not just gambling. He said he had things on people. You know? I mean, he said that he knew things about people, and they had to pay him to keep him quiet. And then he said it. I'd forgotten all about it. I don't know what made me remember it last night, but when I did, it was too late to tell anybody. I could hardly wait until morning to tell you."

"Tell us what, Bonnie'?" said Queenie.

"Well, he said that he knew who it was who killed Bridgit and them. He said he knew who it was. I said that he ought to tell the sheriff, and he just laughed, and then he said a lot of other things, and I just forgot about it. I guess I didn't really believe him. He'd said so much, and he'd been bragging so, and he was so drunk. You know?"

"Back up, Bonnie," said Lottie, "and say it again, slow, just the important part."

"Coker Jack told me that he knew who the killer was."

"Then that's it," said Ellie. "It was the same killer. That's the motive. The killer murdered Coker Jack to protect his identity. That should be all we need to get Richard out. That's a much stronger motive than the one the sheriff says Richard had. Bonnie, you're wonderful."

Ellie jumped up and threw her arms around Bonnie and kissed her.

"I'm going to see Sheriff Kane right now," she added.

"We'll all go," said Lottie. "You might need Bonnie to back you up on this."

Ben Kane was not in his office when the four women arrived. Denver Bond was there, and they went in.

"Denver," said Lottie, "where's Kane?"

"I don't know where he is," said Bond. "He just left me here in charge. What can I do for you?"

"I'm afraid we'll have to talk to the sheriff," said Ellie. "We want to get Richard released."

"Get him released?" said Bond. "How you going to do that?"

"Coker Jack told Bonnie that he knew who killed those three girls," said Ellie. "He also told her that he was blackmailing certain people."

"Oh," said Bond. "That's pretty powerful, all right. You'll have to see Ben. He'll probably be back here pretty soon. You want to wait?"

"I'll wait," said Ellie.

"We'll all wait," said Lottie.

"You want to tell Richard?"

Ellie hesitated a moment and looked at the others.

"Yes," she said, "let's go tell him."

"Only one visitor is allowed back there at a time," said Bond. "Ben's rule."

"You go on back, honey," said Lottie. "We'll wait out here."

Bond unlocked the big door to let Ellie into the hallway of cells, and she walked back to the one where Richard was being kept.

"Richard," she said, "are you all right?"

"I feel better already," he said, "seeing you. I just wish I didn't have to see you here."

"It won't be long," she said. "I have good news. Coker Jack bragged to Bonnie that he knew who had killed the three girls. He also implied that he was blackmailing the man. That means that we know now that there's someone out there who had a stronger motive for killing Coker Jack than you had, and he's already a killer, whoever he is, so he's a much more likely suspect."

"What did Kane say to that?" asked Richard.

"We haven't told him yet," she said. "We're waiting for him to come back to the office."

"We?"

"Lottie and Bonnie and Queenie are out in the office," said Ellie. "They're out there with Denver Bond."

"God, I hope this works," said Richard.

"It's got to," said Ellie, and she put a hand through the bars to touch Richard's cheek. Richard felt the thrill of the touch rush throughout his body. He reached up with his own hand and pressed hers harder against his cheek.

"Ellie," he said, "I love you. You're a wonderful woman. You deserve a lot better than me."

"But you're what I've got," she said with a smile, "and I intend to keep you."

133

Denver Bond stuck his head in the doorway at the far end of the hall.

"Sheriff's back, Ellie," he called.

"Thank you," said Ellie. "I'm coming. Don't worry, Richard. We'll get this all straightened out."

She walked back to the office where Ben Kane had already planted himself in the chair behind his desk. The three working girls were lined up in front of the desk. Bond was standing off to one side. Ellie walked right up to the desk.

"All right," said Kane. "What's this all about?"

"It's about Richard," said Ellie, "my husband."

She hesitated. She wanted to present the information and the argument in just the right way. Everything depended on this presentation.

"You arrested Richard entirely on the basis of circumstantial evidence," she said, "primarily motive. Is that correct?"

"That's right," said Kane.

"We have discovered that someone else in this town is a much more likely suspect, then, because he had a much stronger motive."

"And who would that be?" said Kane. His eyes had narrowed to slits in his wrinkled old face.

"The person who killed the young women," said Ellie. "Coker Jack confided in Bonnie here that he knew the killer's identity. He further implied that he was blackmailing the man."

"Mrs. Fuller," said Kane, "may I make a suggestion?"

"Well, yes."

"If you won't go home and forget all this, then at least go out and hire yourself a good lawyer. Quit running around town playing detective, and find yourself better company to keep."

"Hey," said Queenie.

Denver Bond gritted his teeth.

"But, Sheriff," said Ellie, "what I've just given you is—."

"Hearsay," said Kane. "The word of one unreliable witness reported secondhand by another unreliable witness. A drunken, crooked gambler supposedly said something to a whore."

"Wait a minute, you old son of a bitch," said Queenie.

Kane sprang to his feet and leaned forward across his desk, his face flushed with anger.

"You watch your language," he shouted. "You be careful how you talk to me. Whores. A bunch of whores. Get them out of here, Denver."

"Ben," said Denver, "I think you're wrong. I think you ought to listen—."

"You're not paid to think," snapped Kane. "You're paid to do what I tell you to do. Now get them out of here before I lock them all up."

Chapter Fourteen

Denver Bond escorted the women out onto the sidewalk. He shut the office door behind himself and walked a ways down the street with them.

"He's wrong," he said. "He's just wrong about this."

"Stubborn old bastard," said Queenie.

"He didn't have any business talking to you ladies the way he did," said Bond. "Damn him anyway. I ought to go back in there and quit."

"Don't do that, Denver," said Ellie. "Not yet anyway. I don't want you to lose a job over this, and besides, you might be more help with your badge than without it."

"Maybe you're right," he said.

"Of course she's right," said Lottie. "Just watch your temper. I've never seen you like this."

"It's just that he didn't have any right to talk to you like that," said Denver.

Lottie put a hand on his shoulder.

"Or to you," she said, "but we've got more important things to worry about right now."

"Denver," said Ellie, "will you talk to Richard? I don't think this would be a good time for me to go back in there."

"Sure," he said.

"Tell him what happened with the sheriff, but tell him that we haven't given up."

"Yeah," said Bond. "I'll tell him."

"Thank you," said Ellie.

"But if you don't mind," said Bond, "I think I'll wait a little while and try to cool off some before I go back in there. Right now I feel like punching Ben in the mouth."

"Let's all go have a drink," said Queenie. "I'll buy. I had a busy night last night."

They walked to the Rattlesnake where Queenie bought a bottle. They sat together at a table in a corner. It was still early in the day, and there were few customers in the place. Queenie poured drinks all around.

"No, thank you," said Ellie. "I don't think I should."

"Aw, come on," said Queenie. "You need it worse than the rest of us."

"Don't push it, Queenie," said Lottie. "I'll get you a cup of coffee, honey. You want a cup of coffee?"

"Yes, thank you," said Ellie.

Lottie went after the coffee.

"What'd I say?" said Queenie.

"It's all right," said Ellie. "Really."

Lottie brought the coffee and sat back down.

"Where do we go from here?" said Bonnie.

"We have to find out who the killer is," said Ellie. "That's the only way I can see."

"Okay," said Queenie, "but just how do we do that?"

"I have an idea," said Ellie.

"Well," said Lottie, "let's hear it."

"Did anyone around here know Coker Jack's last name?"

"I don't think so," said Bonnie. "Coker Jack is all I ever heard."

"That's all we got on the paperwork at the sheriff's office," said Bond. "Coker Jack. That's all."

"That's all it says on the marker at Boot Hill," said Lottie.

"Then let's say that it was McKee," said Ellie.

"What?" said Lottie. "McKee? That's your name, honey. At least, it used to be."

"That's right. Let's say his name was McKee, and let's say that I'm his sister. That's how I happened to meet Richard. They're both gamblers. I met Richard through Coker Jack one time up north. Let's say that I have more than one reason to want to know who really killed Coker Jack."

"What good is that going to do?" said Queenie.

"Coker Jack told Bonnie that he knew the killer," said Ellie. "Right? He might have told his sister the same thing. He might even have told her the name."

"Wait a minute," said Bond.

"Let's say that he did," said Ellie. "Let's say that he told me the name. Let's say that I can identify the killer, because Coker Jack, my brother, told me who it is."

"That's setting yourself up as bait," said Bond. "It's too dangerous. The killer will try to kill you."

"And when he does," said Ellie, "we'll know who he is."

"Yeah?" said Queenie. "What if he gets you and nobody sees who done it? What good will that do anyone?"

"Queenie's right," said Bond. "It's just too dangerous. What do you think Richard would say? He wouldn't want you to put yourself in danger to try to save him. You can't do it, Ellie."

"I can't without your help," said Ellie. "All of you. But what other choice do we have? How else are we going to find out who this person is? And if we don't find out who the killer really is, how are we going to save Richard?"

"There's got to be some other way," said Bond.

"Then tell me what it is," said Ellie. "I'll do it."

No one answered. Ellie looked over their faces for a moment.

"That settles it," she said. "I want you, any of you, when you see a chance, to just kind of let it slip out that Coker Jack's name was McKee. Or that you just found out that I'm his sister. Or that you heard somehow that he told me the identity of the killer. Any of that or all of it, depending on the situation. Don't be too obvious about it. We don't want to make anyone suspicious of our motives. Try to make it seem like it just sort of slipped out by mistake. Okay?"

"I still don't like it," said Bond.

"Denver," said Ellie, "if they find Richard guilty and hang him for this murder, you'll be a party to it. You helped to arrest him and keep him in jail, and you know that he's innocent. How will you like that?"

"Damn it," said Bond, "I just wish I could think of another way. Can't we wait a little while and see if we can come up with something else?"

"Wait how long?" said Ellie. "Every day that circuit judge is one day closer."

"She's right," said Queenie. "If we're going to do anything, we got to do it now. And let's not forget, girls. It ain't just Richard Fuller we're trying to save here. If that guy's still in town, any one of us girls might be next."

Bond shot a surreptitious glance at Lottie.

"All right," he said. "I'll go along with it, but I don't think we ought to let Richard know what we're up to here."

"There's no need to let Richard know," said Ellie. "Let's just keep it to ourselves. Just the five of us. And let's get it started as soon as possible."

The train was roaring around a sharp curve in the tracks somewhere in the mountains of the Indian Territory when suddenly the brakes were thrown on, and Sandy was pitched from his seat almost into J.W.'s lap. Other passengers were also tossed about, and there were shouts and curses flung around at nobody in particular in the passenger car. The train came to a complete stop, and passengers were able to regain their proper seats. Some, however, stood up and others looked out the windows. A few made their way to the doors at either end of the car. J.W. McKee was among the boldly curious.

"What the hell's going on here?" he roared.

"We've stopped for some reason, boss," said Sandy.

"God damn it," said J.W., "I can tell that. Where the hell are we?"

Sandy poked his head out the window, then he pulled it back in a hurry. That movement was followed immediately by the sound of a gunshot, and a bullet nicked the train car just above the window.

"It's a holdup, boss," said Sandy.

"God damn it to hell," said J.W. "How many?"

"I seen four out there."

J.W. opened his coat and reached for his long bar-

140

reled Forehand and Wadsworth .44. He quickly checked the cylinder. Sandy followed J.W.'s lead and slipped out his own Smith and Wesson .45. He watched J.W. closely. They still sat in their seats facing each other. Then the door at the far end of the coach, the one J.W. was facing, was thrown open, and a man with a bandanna tied over his face and holding a sawed-off shotgun stepped inside.

"This is a holdup," he shouted. "Just keep your seats and do as you're told and no one will get hurt."

The door at the other end of the coach opened and another bandit stepped in there.

"Do what he says," shouted the second bandit. "You're covered from both ends."

J.W. gave a slight nod while looking into Sandy's eyes, and both men stood up together, raised their right arms almost together and fired, the two shots blending almost into one explosive blast. J.W.'s bullet smashed the sternum of his target, and the man dropped his shotgun and fell backward through the door. Sandy's shot made a hole in the other bandit's forehead. The man's head jerked stupidly back and forth, and then he pitched forward into the aisle. There were screams and shouts from the passengers, and most of them ducked for cover.

"Let's go," said J.W., and he stood up and headed for the far door. Sandy headed for the near door. Sandy had seen four men, so they knew that there were at least two more out there, probably more. It was unlikely that the whole gang had been lined up beside the passenger car. J.W. stepped out on the platform between the cars. Slowly he poked his head around the corner to take a look. An outlaw saw him and raised his gun to fire. J.W. pulled his head back just in time, and the bullet spanged against the corner of the railroad car. But at the far end of the car,

Sandy dropped down to the ground and fired. It was a long pistol shot, and it went wide, but it got the outlaw's attention. As he turned to face this new threat, J.W. looked around the corner again. This time he fired, his bullet tearing into the man's ribs just under the armpit. The man screamed and fell to the ground. J.W. stepped down from the platform, looked in both directions, and walked over to his second victim. The man was still alive. J.W. picked up the man's gun and tossed it away.

He looked around. Where was the other one? And was there only one more? He looked down the tracks toward Sandy, and he saw a man on top of the car raising a revolver toward his foreman.

"Look out," he called, and he fired a shot at the man, but it went wide. Sandy whirled and squeezed off a round which hit the man in the shoulder, causing him to stagger and fall off the car with a shriek. He landed with a dull thud not four feet from where Sandy stood. Sandy checked the man and found him to be unconscious. Still, he tossed the man's gun off out of reach. J.W. walked over to join Sandy.

"That's four," he said, "but there could be more."

"I'll check the other side," said Sandy, and ducked down and went under a coupling to the opposite side of the tracks. He didn't see anyone, but he moved cautiously toward the engine. J.W. was doing the same thing on his side of the train. He had made it about halfway to the engine when the engineer climbed down from his perch, an outlaw right behind him holding a revolver to his head. The outlaw, pushing the engineer along ahead of him, started walking toward J.W. J.W. stopped.

"Toss that gun down, mister," said the outlaw, "or I'll blow his head off."

"Why should I?" said J.W. "I don't know him."

142

The outlaw with the engineer as his shield came closer.

"I mean it," he shouted.

"Go ahead," said J.W., "and then I'll kill you."

"Damn it, mister," said the outlaw, "put your gun down, and I'll let you both live."

"Do I look like that big a fool to you?" said J.W. Then, just as the outlaw stepped past one car, Sandy, from between the cars, raised his arm and took careful aim. He squeezed the trigger of his .45 and sent a bullet into the outlaw's left temple. The man fell without a sound, but the engineer yelled and almost collapsed from fear. He recovered himself and looked at J.W. McKee.

"Would you have let him kill me?" he said.

"We'll never know, will we?" said J.W. "How many of them were there?"

"Five," said the engineer.

"Then we got them all," said J.W. "Why the hell did you stop for them anyway?"

"Just go on up there and see for yourself," said the engineer, still rankling over J.W.'s seeming unconcern for his safety. "The damn tracks are all tore up."

J.W. walked to the front of the engine for a look. Sandy was right behind him.

"Damn," said J.W.

"Boy, howdy," said Sandy. "They did make a mess, didn't they?"

"Damn it to hell," said J.W., and he turned to go after the engineer. He caught up with the man just beyond the rear of the engine. He was talking to the conductor.

"How long will it take to get underway again?" demanded J.W.

"I don't know," said the engineer. "We have to get a crew out here."

"How long will that take?"

"I'm sorry, mister. I just can't say. Someone's going to have to get to the next station. They got a telephone there, and they can call and get a crew out here."

"We'll do her," said J.W. "Come on, Sandy."

J.W. led Sandy to the stock car in which his horses rode. They opened the door and laid out the planks to unload the horses. Then they got out their saddles and saddled all three horses. The engineer ran to the stock car to see what was going on.

"What are you doing?" he said.

"Getting my horses," said J.W. "What the hell does it look like?"

"Why are you unloading them?"

"To get on my way," said J.W. "You sure as hell ain't moving."

"Wait a minute," said the engineer. "You got three horses?"

"That's right."

"Let me send Willie here along with you. You can leave him at the station."

The engineer had indicated the conductor. J.W. looked at the man.

"Climb on then," he said, "and let's get going."

Chapter Fifteen

Ben Kane did not want his particular interest in the activities of Franklin Smith to be generally known. He had questioned Smith once in the presence of witnesses, and that had been enough, perhaps too much. He would not do that again. He would, however, keep his eye on Smith. He had perched himself in a cane-bottomed, straight-backed chair on the wooden sidewalk and leaned back against the facade of the butcher's shop. Across the street was Bubba's cafe, and he had seen Smith go in there just a few minutes before. He would wait and see when Smith came out again and where he went from there. The man was a real puzzle to Ben Kane, and he might well be a threat. Kane had enough problems already.

"Well, is that how you do your job?"

Kane looked to his right to see his son Donald there on the sidewalk.

"How I do my job is my business," said the sheriff.

"You're always nagging at me to go to work," said Donald. "Find me a job like this, and I'll be more than happy to go to work."

"Donald," said Kane, "have you thought any more about going back to college?"

"I never thought about it at all," said Donald. "You

145

were the one who thought about that. Face it, Father. You've raised a son with no ambition."

Across the street, Franklin Smith came out of the cafe. Kane stood up.

"We'll have to take this up later," he said. "I've got to go."

Donald could see that his father was watching something or someone across the street intently. He looked across to see if he could tell what or who it was, and he saw Smith walking toward the hotel. The sheriff stayed on his side of the street, trying not to appear to be dogging the trail of Smith, but Donald thought that he could tell. He did not know Smith, and he was pretty sure that Smith was new in town. He wondered what his father's interest in the man might be. At last he shrugged it off and headed for the Rattlesnake.

Ben Kane followed Smith to the hotel and watched him go inside. He waited a few minutes, then crossed the street and went into the lobby. Smith was nowhere in sight. He must have gone upstairs to his room. Kane walked over to the counter and leaned an elbow on it.

"Hello, Tony," he said. "How're things going?"

Tony Arnall looked up from his paperwork.

"Oh, hi, Sheriff," he said. "Everything's quiet here. Usually is."

"Well," said Kane, "the way things have been around town lately, I just like to keep an eye on things. You see anything suspicious, you let me know."

"Sure," said Arnall, as he watched Kane turn and walk back outside. Kane crossed the street again and lounged against another storefront. He stopped the first handy passerby and engaged him in idle conversation. A few more minutes passed, and Kane began to feel conspicuous. He walked down to Bubba's cafe and went inside. He sat at a table beside the window and ordered a cup of coffee. From where he sat, he could sip his coffee without arousing any suspicion, while watching the front door of the hotel. Kane was only half finished with his coffee when he saw Smith leave the hotel and walk toward the Rattlesnake. He watched and took another sip. Smith went into the saloon. He would probably be there for awhile. Kane paid for his coffee and left.

He walked the long way around to the back of the hotel and let himself in the back door. He moved quickly but quietly, and he managed to get upstairs without being seen. He took a skeleton key out of his vest pocket and unlocked the door to Smith's room, then went inside and shut the door. He stood there for a moment looking the room over. It looked about like what he would have expected, except for the table which was covered with papers. Kane went to the table and sat down. There were pages of notes with the names of the murdered women on them. There were notes with the answers to questions he had asked of people around town. Who was the first one killed? When did it happen? How had the bodies been discovered? Who had discovered them? One particularly interesting piece of paper was headed, "What has the sheriff done?"

Kane rummaged through the papers some more, and he found a letter written on letterhead stationery. It was addressed to Mr. Franklin Smith, and it was from an editor at *The Police Gazette*.

"A reporter," Kane said out loud in a harsh whisper. He read quickly a few more of Smith's notes, and then he got up hurriedly and left the room. He went out of the hotel the same way he had gone in. He got back out on the main street, looked around, hitched up his britches by the waistband and started walking casually back toward his office. Gospel Bill was dancing around in the middle of the street out in front of the

Rattlesnake and preaching in his stentorious, though raspy, voice. A small crowd had gathered there to watch and to listen, mostly for the pure entertainment value. The grins on their faces betrayed this attitude. There were a couple of prim and proper ladies standing apart from the disrespectful crowd, listening intently and nodding their heads in solemn and profound agreement. Ben Kane stopped on the sidewalk to listen. Gospel Bill looked the same as always. His hair was wild, his one suit rumpled. He was spotted all over with dirt and bits of grass, and his worn old Bible flapped limply in his left hand.

"The word of the Lord came again unto me," Gospel Bill bellowed, "saying:

"Son of man, there were two women, the daughters of one mother:

"And they committed whoredoms in Egypt; they committed whoredoms in their youth: there were their breasts pressed, and there they bruised the teats of their virginity.

"And the names of them were Aholah the elder, and Aholibah her sister: and they were mine, and they bare sons and daughters."

He slapped the withered old book with its faded black cover and then raised it high over his head.

"It's all right here in the good book, God's own word," he declared. "And it's for all times and it's for all places. It's for Egypt and it's for Jerusalem and, yea, even unto us right here and now, it's for our own sinful little town of Jubilation in the dry and barren and windswept plains of western Texas, the great and sovereign state of Texas. Amen. For they committed whoredoms in Jubilation. And they committed whoredoms in their youth in the Rattlesnake Saloon. Verily and truthfully and undeniably, I tell ye they did, and so do they still."

"Amen, brother," said Kane. A cowboy rode up to dismount and tie his horse at the hitch rail in front of the Rattlesnake.

"And Aholah played the harlot when she was mine," blared Gospel Bill, "and she doted on her lovers, on the Assyrians her neighbors,

"Which were clothed blue, captains and rulers, all of them desirable young men, horsemen riding upon horses."

The cowboy looked at Gospel Bill. He started to go on into the saloon, but his eye caught the two prim ladies and the stern looking sheriff. He hesitated.

"Thus she committed her whoredoms with them," Gospel Bill continued, "with all them that were the chosen men of Assyria, and with all on whom she doted: with all their idols she defiled herself.

"Neither left she her whoredoms brought from Egypt: for in her youth they lay with her, and they bruise the breasts of her virginity, and poured their whoredom upon her.

"Wherefore I have delivered her into the hand of her lovers, into the hand of the Assyrians, upon whom she doted.

"These discovered her nakedness: they took her sons and daughters, and slew her with the sword: and she became famous among women; for they had executed judgment upon her."

A chill crept up the spine of Ben Kane, and the horse at the rail spewed forth a stream of steaming piss. One of the drunken cowboys turned to his buddy.

"Say, pard," he said, "let's go on back inside and see if we can't uncover some nakedness."

"Commit some whoredoms?" said the other.

"Hell, yes, and bruise some teats."

They headed for the front door of the Rattlesnake, and Kane scowled fiercely and walked on toward his office.

"Hey, Lottie," yelled Queenie from halfway up the stairs, "have you seen Lola?"

Lottie was standing at the bar visiting with Arch. She looked toward Queenie on the stairway.

"No," she said. "Have you checked her room?"

"I knocked on the door," said Queenie. "She don't answer."

Bonnie was sitting at a table not far from where Lottie stood. She turned into the conversation.

"I haven't seen Lola all day today, come to think of it," she said.

There was a moment of tense silence. Lottie looked from Queenie to Bonnie. When she started moving, she moved fast.

"Come on," she said.

Lottie had caught up to Queenie before Queenie could turn around, and Bonnie was coming up right behind the two of them. They rushed on up to the top of the stairs and down the hall to Lola's room. Lottie pounded hard on the door.

"Lola," she called out. "Lola. Are you in there?"

There was no answer. Lottie looked back at the other two girls.

"You haven't seen her all day?" she said.

"No," said Bonnie.

"I ain't seen her," said Queenie. "Oh, my God."

Lottie tried to open the door, but it was locked. She pushed on it, and bashed it with her shoulder.

"Here," said Queenie, holding out a skeleton key. "Wait a minute. Try my key."

Lottie took the key and fumbled with it for a few seconds. Her hands were trembling. At last she got the key in the lock and turned it. She twisted the doorknob and shoved open the door. Then she gasped. Queenie shoved her aside and stepped into the room.

"Oh, God," she said. A hand went to her mouth, and she turned her face to the wall. Bonnie stood in the doorway as if in a trance. There on the bed, Lola was lying on her back on top of the bedclothes. She was naked. Her legs were straight and together, and her arms were straight by her sides. Her eyes were closed, and her face seemed calm enough, but the overall serenity of the scene was marred by a frightening gash across her throat. The bedclothes under her neck and shoulder were soaked in blood already dry and dark. Against the darkness of the blood, her body appeared to be almost as white as fresh fallen snow. Bonnie started to sob convulsively.

"Go on," said Lottie. "Get out of here."

She shoved the other two girls out into the hallway.

"Take her downstairs and get her a glass of brandy," she said to Queenie. "And tell Arch to run over to the sheriff's office. Go on. Hurry."

Queenie took Bonnie by the arm and started for the stairs, and Lottie stepped back into the room. She stood for a moment looking at the remains of her friend. Then she shut the door, and sat down in a chair to wait.

Smith was sitting at the bar having a cup of coffee when the two near hysterical women came down the stairs.

"Arch," said Queenie, "give us a couple of brandies. Hurry it up."

Arch put two glasses on the bar and then shoved a bottle toward Queenie.

"What's the matter with you two?" he said.

A few feet down the bar, Smith was watching with interest.

"Arch," said Queenie, after she had taken a quick

swallow of brandy, "go get the sheriff."

"What is it?" said Arch.

"It's Lola," said Queenie. "Go get Kane. Hurry it up, will you?"

Arch ran out from behind the bar and out into the street. He was running down the street toward the sheriff's office when he saw Kane headed the same way. He ran up to Kane and accosted him in the street.

"Sheriff," he said. "Come quick. The Rattlesnake. There's been another one."

Kane grabbed Arch by the shirt front and shoved him against the wall.

"Keep your voice down, Arch," he said. "Calm down."

He glanced up and down the street. A few people were looking. He released Arch and stepped back. The onlookers went on about their business.

"Now," said Kane, keeping his voice low. "Another what?"

"It's Lola, Sheriff," said Arch. "The girls, Bonnie and Queenie, they came down and said I should come and get you."

"Murdered?" said Kane.

"I took it that way," said Arch. "I didn't go up and look. I just came straight after you."

"All right," said Kane. "Let's walk back over to the Rattlesnake, and let's act like there's nothing wrong. I don't want to draw a crowd."

They found Lottie still sitting in the room.

"Is this the way you found her?" said Kane.

"Yeah," said Lottie. "Just like the others."

"You touched anything?"

"Are you kidding?"

"Don't get smart," said Kane. "Just answer the questions."

"No," said Lottie. "I didn't touch nothing."

152

"When did you discover the body?"

"Just now. Just — five minutes ago. I don't know. We found her, and I sent them after you."

"Who actually made the discovery?" said Kane.

"Me and Bonnie and Queenie," said Lottie. "I was downstairs at the bar. Queenie yelled down and asked me if I'd seen Lola. I hadn't. Then Bonnie said she hadn't seen her all day. That got us worried, and we came up here and knocked. When she didn't answer, we opened the door and looked in. I sent them on downstairs. Told them to send Arch after you. That's all."

Kane walked over to the bed and looked down at the naked body. He stared at it, Lottie thought, for a long time. She wanted to call him a dirty old bastard, but she didn't. She wanted to get up and cover Lola, but she didn't do that either.

"How long is this going to go on?" she said. "Till we're all dead? When are you going to catch the son of bitch who's doing this?"

"We're doing all we can," said Kane. "You're in a business that attracts men like that. Don't blame me if you attract them faster than I can track down a killer."

"Oh, God," said Lottie. "Can I go now?"

"Go on," said Kane. "I'll have more questions for all of you later. Go on for now."

Lottie got up and walked out into the hallway. She almost ran into Franklin Smith who was walking toward the room.

"Excuse me," said Smith. Lottie walked around him and went down the stairs, and Smith walked on to the open door. He stepped into the doorway and looked at the body on the bed. Kane was still standing in the same spot, apparently unaware of Smith's arrival.

"And she committed whoredoms in her youth," he said, "and they slew her with the sword. Amen."

Smith cleared his throat loudly and conspicuously, and Kane's head jerked toward the noise.

"Smith," he said, "what are you doing here?"

"The same thing you are, Sheriff," said Smith. "What was her name?"

"You get out of here," said Kane. "I could arrest you for interfering with a lawman in the line of his duty."

"It sounded more like a scripture reading I interrupted," said Smith.

"Get on out of here," said Kane, and his hard look was as convincing as were his words.

"All right," said Smith. "I've seen enough anyway."

He turned and went back downstairs. Lottie, Bonnie and Queenie were seated together at a table near the bar. Arch was back behind the bar pouring himself a drink. Smith walked over to the table.

"May I join you ladies?" he said.

"Sit down," said Lottie.

"It must have been an awful thing for you," said Smith, "finding her like that. What was her name?"

"We just called her Lola," said Bonnie. "That's all. Just Lola."

"I guess, then," Smith said, "there's no family to be notified."

"No," said Queenie. "No family. None of us has got any family, mister. It's better that way."

"The way she is up there," said Smith. "Is that just the way—the others were found?"

"Just like that," said Lottie "Just the same."

"And there are no clues? The sheriff doesn't have any suspects at all?"

"Not a God damn thing," said Queenie. "Can you believe that? Four girls killed like that, and he hasn't done a damn thing."

"Take it easy, Queenie," said Lottie, and she put a hand on Queenie's arm.

154

"Tell me about your Sheriff Kane," said Smith. "What kind of a man is he?"

"Pig headed," said Bonnie.

"Just a pig," said Queenie.

"I just overheard him quoting scripture beside the body," said Smith.

"I'm not surprised," said Lottie. "He's like that. He ain't quite as bad as Gospel Bill, I guess, but then, that's Gospel Bill's job, ain't it? Yeah, Ben's a Bible thumper. He thinks we're all going straight to hell. I wonder sometimes if he really gives a damn about finding that killer."

"He probably thinks we all deserve to have our throats cut," said Queenie. "Send us to hell that much sooner."

"He probably does," said Bonnie, "but I think he just does that, all that holy talk, you know, to kind of make up for his boy."

"What do you mean?" said Smith.

"Well, Donald's in here most every night," said Bonnie, "drinking and gambling and — ."

"And other things," said Queenie suggestively.

"Knock it off," said Lottie. "He's coming down."

Smith glanced toward the stairway. The sheriff had stopped about halfway down for an instant when he saw Smith sitting at the table with the remaining working girls. Then he walked on down and went over to the table. He stood there for a moment.

"Smith," he said, "I want to talk to you."

"Sure," said Smith. "What is it?"

"Let's take a walk," said Kane.

Chapter Sixteen

Kane led Smith to the sheriff's office, but once there, he did not go in. He opened the door and stuck his head inside.

"Denver," he said.

"Yes, sir?"

"There's been another killing over at the Rattlesnake."

"God," said Bond. "Who?"

"The one they call Lola."

Bond breathed a sigh of relief. His heart was pounding with fright.

"Lola," he repeated.

"Get over there and take care of things," said Kane. "Have the body taken care of. Ask all the usual questions. You know what to do."

"Yes, sir," said Bond.

Kane closed the door and continued walking, and Smith walked alongside.

"Where are we going, Sheriff," said Smith.

"Someplace private," said Kane.

Smith gave a shrug of his broad shoulders.

"All right, Sheriff," he said. "Lead the way."

Denver Bond walked fast. He had to hold himself back to keep from running over to the Rattlesnake Saloon. When he went in through the front doors, he saw Lottie right away. She was still with the other girls there at the table. Bond rushed right over to her.

"Lottie," he said, "are you all right?"

"Yeah," she said. "I'm okay. A little shaky is all. But, God, Denver, it's awful."

"I know, Lottie," he said. "I know. The rest of you girls all right?"

They each nodded their assent. Bonnie started sobbing again, and Queenie lit a ready roll cigarette. Bond pulled out a chair and sat down with the girls. Then he motioned for Arch to come over and join them. He had been through this three times before with Kane, and he knew all the questions to ask. Who discovered the body and when? When was the last time anyone had seen Lola? Had anyone seen anyone or anything suspicious? Who was the last person known to have been with Lola? Did anyone hear anything? Did anyone know if Lola had a last name or any family to be notified? Was anything out of place in her room? Had anything been stolen? The answers to the questions were as disappointing in this latest case as they had been in the previous three. There were no leads, no clues, no ideas, no trails to follow. Bond went upstairs to look at the body and the scene of the crime, more out of a sense of duty than anything else. Looking at the grisly sight did not do him any good. He knew no more after having viewed it than he had before. He went back downstairs.

"Arch," he said, "is anybody upstairs?"

"Not a living soul," said Arch. His face turned a bit

red when he realized what he had said. "I mean, no. No one's up there."

"Well, don't let anyone up there," said Bond. "Not until the body's been removed. I mean, no one."

"I got you," said Arch.

"I've got to go over and get Mort Sexton to come and take care of the body. You want to walk over with me, Lottie?"

"Yeah," said Lottie. "Someone needs to make funeral arrangements."

"You set it all up, Lottie," said Queenie. "We'll help you pay for it. Just like before."

"Yeah," said Bonnie. "She's got to have a funeral."

"Y'all just set tight," said Bond, "until Mort gets over here and gets done. Me and Lottie will be back soon, too."

They walked outside and started toward Sexton's Undertaking Establishment. Bond took hold of Lottie's arm.

"When Ben stuck his head in the office and told me to get over here," he said, "he like to scared me to death. He said there's been another killing at the Rattlesnake. He didn't say who was the victim. I'm sorry about Lola, Lottie, truly I am, but God, I was scared for you."

They walked on a few more steps with no words.

"Let me take you away from there," Bond said, and his voice was pleading. "Marry me, Lottie."

"Denver," said Lottie. "Not now."

"But it's the only way I can protect you, Lottie. Can't you see that? I can't protect you twenty-four hours a day in the Rattlesnake."

"You couldn't protect me twenty-four hours a day in your own house, Denver. Would you quit your job and sit home all the time?"

"This killer is not striking women in their homes,"

158

said Bond. "He's attacking women at the Rattlesnake. He's not going after men's wives, he — ."

"I know," said Lottie. "He's killing whores. Damn it, I can't leave Bonnie and Queenie in danger. I can't just run out on them, and I can't marry you just to get your protection from this killer."

"It's not just that," said Bond. "I love you, Lottie. This other business just makes it more — you know, urgent."

"Here's Mort's place," said Lottie. "We going in?"

Kane led Smith around behind the hotel. No one was back there, even though the street out front was as busy as usual.

"Wait for me here," said Kane. "I'll be right back."

"What are we — ?"

"I'll just be a minute," said the sheriff, and he turned and walked back around the building, leaving Smith standing there alone and perplexed. But the reporter's curiosity won out, and Smith waited, wondering what the sheriff might be up to. It had to have something to do with the investigation of the murders of the prostitutes. Kane and Smith had nothing else in common, nothing else to discuss. Soon, Kane returned. He was driving a buggy. He pulled up beside where Smith was waiting.

"Climb in," he said. Smith got in and sat beside Kane, and Kane drove down the backstreet and out of town. He said nothing, just kept driving.

"Sheriff," said Smith. "Where are we going?"

"You'll see soon enough," said Kane.

Smith turned to look over his shoulder, and he saw the town of Jubilation getting smaller and smaller behind him.

"If you're looking for a private place to talk," he

said, "I think we've gone far enough out of town."

"Not quite," said Kane.

He drove on farther, and finally he turned off the road and headed down into a creek bed. In the middle of the creek, he stopped.

"What the hell are you up to?" said Smith.

"You couldn't take my advice," said Kane, "could you? You had to keep poking around in it?"

"What are we out here for?"

Kane unbuttoned his coat to reveal a 1878 model Colt .45 with a short four-inch barrel.

"What are you doing?" said Smith. "Did you bring me out here to kill me?"

Kane reached for the revolver, and Smith screamed and jumped from the buggy into the creek.

"No!" Smith shouted, and the shout frightened the horse. It bolted forward, and Kane grabbed for the reins. Smith slipped in the creek and fell to his knees, but he scrambled to his feet and ran. The horse was trying to climb up the bank on the opposite side of the creek, but the bank on that side was steeper than the one he had come down. He struggled and slipped, almost falling. Kane was lashing at him with the reins, trying to regain control. Smith ran down the center of the creek for about ten yards, then came out of the water on the side of the creek opposite Kane. Kane yelled at the horse and lashed at it, and the animal veered to its left and fell, pulling the buggy over with it. Kane flew out with a roar and landed with a splash in the shallow water. He struggled to his feet, looked down the creek in the direction in which Smith had run. Then he looked at the wretched horse, trying to regain its feet. He wanted Smith, but he didn't want to walk back to town either. He moved to the horse and grabbed it by the headstall and heaved and pulled, trying to help the animal to its feet. He finally succeeded, but the buggy was still on its side. Well, it would wait. It would also keep the horse from going anywhere.

He pulled the .45 out of its holster and started after Smith. The man had a good lead on him. In fact, Kane could not even see Smith. He thought that Smith had headed back toward the town, but he had been so busy with the frightened horse that he wasn't even sure of that. He ran a few yards down the creek and then climbed up the bank to look across the flat prairie. There he was, running. Kane lifted the Colt and took aim. He held it for a moment, then lowered it again. It was too long a shot for a handgun, especially for his short-barreled Colt. He started running after his prey.

Smith ran for his life. He ran with his head high, and he took long, high strides. He sucked in deep breaths through his nostrils, and he exhaled through his mouth. He ran with desperation, and he felt his heart pounding in his chest as it heaved in and out. Each time one of his feet pounded on the ground, he felt it jar his entire large frame. And still he ran. The town still looked small off in the distance, but he knew that he could make it. He could run that far. He had to run that far.

Behind him Kane was running, but Kane was older. Kane had not run more than six steps for a good many years. His belly sagged over his belt, and he could feel it flopping as he ran. He found it more and more difficult to breathe, and then he felt a sharp pain in his chest. He ran a few more steps, and then he slowed to a walk and then he stopped. He could not catch the man on foot. He stood panting, gasping for breath. He lifted his Colt again and aimed at the fleeing man. It was as long a shot as before, but he tried it anyway. He couldn't catch the man, so he tried the shot. He pulled the trigger, and the blast echoed across the empty, flat prairie, but Smith kept running. Kane turned and

161

started walking back toward the creek.

When he arrived back at the creek bank and started down, he slipped and fell, rolling all the way down into the creek. He groaned with pain as he struggled back to his feet, and then he waded through the water back to the horse and the capsized buggy. It took awhile, and he was afraid for his heart as he pushed and strained to upright the vehicle, but he finally got the job done. The reins were tangled, and it took him a few minutes to get them back in order. Then he led the horse around and back through the creek to the bank on the other side. He started to climb into the seat, but he lacked the strength. He stood there, leaning on the buggy and breathing heavily for another long moment. Then he tried again. This time he made it. He gave the reins a snap and started after Smith. Smith was far ahead by this time, but Jubilation was farther yet. Kane was glad that he had taken the man so far out of town. He snapped the reins again to pick up speed. As the horse ran faster, Kane could tell that he was closing the distance between him and Smith. He lashed at the horse impatiently. Smith still ran.

The horse was practically on him before Smith heard the pounding hooves, and he turned his head to look over his shoulder. As he did, he stumbled, and he sprawled headlong on the ground, rolling as he hit. Kane couldn't stop the buggy in time. He raced past Smith. Smith scrambled to his feet, but by then, Kane had managed to stop the buggy. He pulled out his Colt and turned in the seat to fire. The bullet tore through Smith's left shoulder.

"Ah!" he screamed in pain. "Are you crazy?"

He turned to run again, and Kane fired a second shot. This one hit Smith in the left thigh, and he stumbled and fell again. He rolled over to face his attacker.

"You are crazy," he shouted. "You're crazy."

162

Kane climbed down out of the buggy and walked toward Smith.

"Why are you doing this?" said Smith.

Kane walked closer.

"Damn it, man," shouted Smith. "Why?"

Kane raised the Colt once more and aimed for Smith's heart.

"No!" screamed Smith, and Kane pulled the trigger. The shot was true, and Smith lay dead on the bleak and lonesome prairie. Kane reloaded the revolver, then walked back to the buggy. He climbed into the seat and started the drive back to town. He did not look back.

He delivered the horse and buggy back to the stable, and Gifford Vile, the stableman came running.

"Where the hell have you been with that?" he said.

Kane dropped the reins and climbed slowly and painfully down.

"It's all muddy, and the upholstery is torn," said Vile. "Look at this here singletree. It's cracked. Split. That son of a bitch will break right in half. It's going to have to be replaced. Ben, what — ?"

"Just send me the bill," said Kane, and he turned and walked away. He walked the distance back to his house and went inside where he dropped heavily into his favorite chair. He was sitting there breathing heavily, staring at the wall in front of him, when Donald walked in. The young man stopped and stared at his father for a moment. Old Kane's boots were caked with mud, and mud was on his clothes. He was wet all over, and his face and hands were scuffed.

"What the hell have you been into?" said Donald.

Kane looked up at his son, but he did not respond.

"You look awful," said Donald. "What have you been doing? Where have you been?"

"Never mind where I've been," said Kane. "You just worry about where you're going with your life. That's enough for you to worry about."

"Oh, come on, Father. You come home looking like that, filthy and muddy and ragged. You look like you've been dragged behind a horse, through cow shit or something, and you won't tell me anything about it. You don't expect me to be curious?"

"Be curious all you want," said Kane. "You can stay curious. And watch your language in this house. You know how I feel about that."

"And you know how I feel about it," shouted Donald. "To hell with it, and to hell with you. I don't give a God damn where you've been anyway."

Kane heaved himself up out of his chair and took a faltering step toward Donald.

"You don't know," he said, his voice shaking with rage, his right hand pointing a trembling finger at his son's face. "You just don't know what I'd do for you. What I've done for you. You. You've been my whole life. Everything has been for you. It's all been for you. And you don't even know it. You don't want it. You sneer at it. Donald, son, it's all been for you."

Chapter Seventeen

Ben Kane nearly wore himself out again railing at his son. When he finally stopped, he stood panting in the middle of the floor. Donald knew that he had almost pushed the old man too far.

"All right," he said. "All right. Calm down. I didn't mean to get you so excited. Listen. I heard something down at the Rattlesnake just now. You know that gambler that got himself killed? Coker Jack?"

"What about him?" said Kane.

"Well, it seems he had a last name after all. McKee."

"McKee?"

"That's right," said Donald. "And he had a sister."

"A sister?" said Kane. "You mean—?"

"Ellie McKee," said Donald. "Mrs. Fuller. It seems that Fuller and Coker Jack McKee were old acquaintances. From the professional gamblers' circuit, I expect. Mrs. Fuller met her husband through her brother somewhere up north."

165

"Coker Jack and Fuller didn't let on that they knew each other," said Kane.

"It's an old ploy, Father," said Donald. "They were probably cheating together. As a team. One wins and the other loses. They split the winnings later on in private."

Kane began pacing the floor, thoughtfully rubbing his chin.

"Wait a minute," he said. "Wait a minute. What about the night that Coker Jack got killed? The card game earlier that night? Fuller accused Coker Jack of cheating, right there in front of everyone. What about that? Then they pulled guns on each other. What about that, huh?"

"I don't know," said Donald. "I'm just telling you what I heard down at the Rattlesnake. But it is interesting, isn't it?"

"How? What do you mean?"

"No one fired a shot. It made a good show."

"But if you're right," said Kane, "that would mean that I've got the wrong man in jail. Wouldn't it?"

"Oh," said Donald, "not necessarily. There could have been a falling out among thieves later. Something like that. Maybe they got into a fight over the split."

"Yeah," said Kane. "It could have happened that way. Yeah. Where did you say you heard this?"

"Down at the Rattlesnake," said Donald, "but all I heard is that Coker Jack's name was McKee and that he had a sister. The rest is speculation."

"Yeah," said Kane. "Yeah, I know that. Who'd you hear it from?"

"Those whores that Mrs. Fuller has been hanging around. I wonder if she's going to go into the business after they hang her husband. That would be interesting, wouldn't it?"

Donald chuckled at the thought.

"Oh, yes," he said. "There was one other thing."

"What?" said Kane. "What was it?"

"They said that Coker Jack knew who the killer of the whores was."

"They already tried that one on me," said Kane, "trying to make me turn Fuller loose."

"But they said that he had told his sister. Do you believe that? Why hasn't she come to you with the information? It's all very curious, isn't it?"

"Yes," said Kane, "it is. I've got to have another talk with that woman and get to the bottom of all this."

"Oh, Father," said Donald. "Why don't you clean up first. You really don't want to go around looking like that."

"Yeah," said Kane, grumbling. "I will."

"And one other thing," said Donald.

"What?"

"I really need some money. Could you let me have a few dollars?"

Kane reached almost automatically into his back pocket and pulled out a wallet. He opened it up and pulled out some bills which he handed to his son.

"Thanks, Father," said Donald. "I'll see you later. Okay?"

It had been a hard ride to the end of the track, and when they dismounted in front of the railroad depot, J.W. sent Sandy down the street to the stable they had passed on the way in. Sandy was to get the horses pampered a bit after their strenuous trip, walk them around, feed them some oats and brush them down. J.W. went into the depot with the conductor and waited while the man made his report and the station agent cranked the telephone and made a call to get a work crew sent to repair the tracks and rescue the stranded train. Then he asked the agent about his daughter. Given the dates and the fact that she was a young woman traveling alone, the agent finally remembered Ellie.

"She asked me where the stage depot was at," he said, "and I told her. I guess she went down there and caught a stage."

J.W. went to the stage station where he found out that Ellie had caught a stage to a town further south. It was called Jubilation.

"How long a ride is it?" he asked.

"Well," said the agent, "it takes our coaches two days. They stop overnight at a place along the way called Dog Track."

J.W. thanked the man and went back to the railroad depot where he sent a telegraph message to his wife.

HAVE TRACKED ELLIE TO JUBILATION TX. WE ARE ON OUR WAY THERE ON HORSEBACK. DON'T WORRY. WE'LL BRING HER BACK SAFE.

From there he walked on to the stable to get Sandy. The foreman had just about finished with the horses.

"We've got another long stretch ahead of us," said J.W. "Let's get us a good meal under our belts before we start."

168

They found a cafe where they could order steaks, and they were pleasantly surprised to discover that the quality of the steaks as well as the preparation was good. They ate well, knowing that it would be their last good meal for awhile. The stagecoach, J.W. had been told, took two days to make the trip to Jubilation. J.W. figured that he and Sandy could make it in a day. They followed the meal with one shot of good whiskey apiece, and then they walked back to the stable for the horses. They saddled all three animals and then mounted up, Sandy leading Sampson. They followed the stagecoach road, and as soon as the town had vanished in the background, they could see nothing except the vast prairie around them, the road upon which they traveled marking a long, seemingly endless scar across its back.

Denver Bond unlocked the big door and walked down the hallway to Richard Fuller's cell. Fuller should have finished his meal, and Bond was going to retrieve the tray. It was part of the dull routine of his job whenever there was a prisoner in the jail. As he approached the cell, he could see the tray on the floor near the bars where Fuller had placed it after finishing.

"All done, Richard?" he said. He knew the answer to the question. It was just something to say.

"Yeah. It wasn't bad today," said Fuller.

"Would you come over here and kick that thing out here so I can pick it up?" said Bond.

Fuller walked over to the tray and gave it a shove with his foot. He pushed it out under the bars into the hallway, but he pushed it out to Bond's left. He did that deliberately. Bond was standing close to the bars, and when he bent to pick up the tray, he leaned to his left. That exposed his right side to the bars. Richard reached through the bars and jerked the gun out of Bond's holster. Bond straightened up in a hurry.

"Hey," he said.

The revolver was aimed at his chest, and Fuller thumbed back the hammer.

"Don't make me use this, Denver," said Fuller. "Unlock this damn cell door."

"Aw, Richard," said Bond, his voice whining.

"Just unlock it."

"All right," said Bond. "I'll do it. Just don't point that thing at me. Okay? You don't have to point that thing at me."

He unlocked the cell door, and Fuller stepped out into the hallway.

"I can't stay in here," he said. "Not with Ellie out there trying to find a killer. I can't just sit there doing nothing."

"Wait a minute," said Bond. "At least hit me or something. Make it look good."

"I can't hit you, Denver," said Fuller. "Hell, I like you."

"You threatened to shoot me."

"Aw, that was just a show. You wouldn't have let me out otherwise. Would you?"

"Well, I guess not, but, damn it, Richard, you're just going to walk out of here. I'm the one who's got to face Kane."

"Just tell him what happened," said Fuller. "Tell him I got the drop on you."

"Sure," said Bond. "Sure. Hey, wait a minute."

"What do you mean wait? I've got to get out of

170

here. What if the sheriff comes back?"

"I've got to tell you something now that you've broke jail."

"All right," said Fuller, "but hurry it up. What is it?"

"Ellie's set herself up as bait to catch the killer."

"What? How'd she do that?"

"She's had the girls at the Rattlesnake spread it around that Coker Jack was her brother, and that he told her who the killer was."

"Oh, my God," said Richard. "I've got to find her."

"You can't just go running around town," said Bond. "Where are you going?"

"I—I don't know."

"Go to my house."

"What?"

"What better place is there?" said Bond. "Who would ever think to look for an escapee in the deputy sheriff's house?"

"Yeah," said Fuller. "Maybe you're right."

"I'll let Ellie know where you're at," said Bond. "Maybe she can sneak around to see you there."

"Okay," said Fuller. "Thanks."

He turned and ran down the hallway toward the office, but he stopped at the door and turned back around.

"Hey," he said. "Where do you live?"

Bond gave Fuller directions to his house at the far end of a Jubilation side street.

"Watch yourself," he said. "Don't let anyone see you, and for God's sake, go out the back door."

Fuller left the jail by the back door, and Bond stood alone in the hallway beside the empty cell. He tried to think of a way to explain to the sheriff how he had let the prisoner escape, how he had let the man get the drop on him. He had violated several of Kane's procedural rules, and he had known at the time that he was doing so, but he had gotten to know Richard and to like and trust him, so he had been careless. In the first place, he had carried the keys with him down the hallway. He was not supposed to do that unless he intended to open the cell. In the second place, he had not made Richard go to the far side of the cell while he stood close to the bars to pick up the tray. He could think of no way to explain what had happened without admitting that he had violated those rules.

"Damn," he said.

Kane might tend to be a little easier on him if it appeared that Fuller had used violence, but Fuller had refused to hit him. He paced up and down the hallway, wondering when the sheriff might return. At last he threw up his arms in a gesture of resignation.

"Oh, hell," he said, and he walked into the cell just vacated by Fuller and over to the concrete wall. He placed both hands on the wall, one on either side of his head. He took a deep breath, closed his eyes, gritted his teeth, and bashed his head into the wall.

"Ow."

He staggered back a few steps and stood there weaving and feeling slightly dizzy, slightly nauseous. Then he moved over to the cot and lay down on his back to groan.

Fuller made it to the house all right and let himself in the back door. Bond had told them that he would find the back door unlocked. He had skulked along the back roads and alleyways, occasionally pressing himself sneakily against the back walls of buildings, but he had seen surprisingly few people out and about, and those he had seen had apparently not noticed him. If they had, they did not recognize him or did not care. His heart was pounding with excitement, and he knew that it would take him a few minutes to calm down. He had never been a fugitive before. He had never broken out of jail before. In fact, he reminded himself, he had never before been in jail. Then he remembered something else. He had never before had a wife and a child on the way. It was amazing how much his life had changed in just a few short days. He found a chair and sat down.

What now? he asked himself. What now? Was he really safe in this house? Did Bond get many visitors? Had Fuller really managed to enter the house unseen? And what about Bond, himself? He liked Bond, and Bond seemed to like him, but Bond was, after all, a lawman. Would friendship or sense of duty win out? Fuller felt a little guilty being suspicious of Bond, but he felt a little foolish trusting the man. But if he decided to leave Bond's house, where would he go? Where else in Jubilation would he be safe? He thought about going to the hotel to find Ellie. Then the two of them could ride out of town. But he quickly rejected that plan. In the first place, he had no way of knowing that Ellie would be in her room just then. And even if he succeeded in finding her, he couldn't be sure that he could secure two horses and get them safely out of town. He had tried once before to leave town by himself, and he had been caught. And even if he did manage to locate Ellie and two horses and to get out of town, Ellie would be with him on the outlaw trail. He couldn't drag her into that kind of life, even if she were not in her delicate condition. He was at a loss. He did not know what to do. He decided to settle down and wait and to trust Denver Bond.

Chapter Eighteen

Kane flew into a towering rage, and when he had worn himself out and run out of things to say, he paused and took three deep breaths. He gave Bond a final hard look.

"Go get that head taken care of," he said.

"I'm all right," said Bond.

"You sure?"

"Yeah."

"In that case, get out and get together a posse. We're going after Fuller right now. No one has ever escaped from my jail, and I'm not about to let that tinhorn gambler be the first. Get them together and bring them back here."

Bond left the office, and Kane busied himself with gathering up guns and ammunition for the chase. It occurred to him that if the posse had cause to ride out in the direction in which he had left Smith's body, he would be able to blame that killing, too, on Fuller. That thought helped to calm him down a little. It wasn't long before Bond returned with a dozen mounted men in the street in front of the office. Kane stepped out on the sidewalk.

"You're all deputized," he said, "and I want you to behave like deputies. Anyone who's not properly armed, come inside the office to get a weapon."

Several men went inside to arm themselves, and Bond made notes of who took what to be sure that the weapons would all be returned when the search was over. Then they gathered in the street again.

"First thing we do is search this town from one end to the other," said Kane. "Denver, you organize the hunt. I want every building and every house searched. If we don't find him in town, then we look for tracks that show that he left town. Ask every citizen to account for his horse. Check the stable. Now get it going."

Soon Denver Bond had men going up and down the streets of Jubilation, looking and asking questions. He made sure that he, himself, was among the party that searched his own street, and when they reached his house, he issued orders.

"You two look over there," he said. "This here's my house. I'll just give it a quick look-see."

He went inside and found Fuller in a corner with his revolver in his hand.

"What's going on out there?" said Fuller.

"A house to house search," said Bond. "We're looking for you. Ain't seen a sign of you. Sit tight. I'll see you later."

He went back outside to join the rest of his group. It was two hours before the posse had regrouped in front of the sheriff's office.

"There's no sign of him in town," said Bond, "and we can't find anywhere he might have got a horse."

"If he's not in town," said Kane, "he had to have left, and if he left, he had to have a horse. Split this posse into four groups. I want one to ride out each direction. Look for Fuller or for any sign that might be Fuller's. Anyone who finds anything, fire three quick shots. The rest of us will come running. Let's go."

Kane led his group in the same direction in which he had taken Franklin Smith in the buggy.

When Kane left her room at the hotel, Ellie walked over to the Rattlesnake. She found Lottie standing at the bar talking to Arch.

"Richard has escaped," she said.

"I know," said Lottie. "Kane was in here, too. He searched the whole place. Every room. He practically accused us of hiding him in here somewhere."

"That's the same way he talked to me," said Ellie. "I wonder where he's gone to."

"There's no telling," said Lottie.

"I don't see how he can get away," said Arch. "Kane's got the whole male population out looking. All except me, I guess."

"Why did Richard do that?" said Ellie. "Why couldn't he have had more patience? This will only convince the sheriff the more that Richard is guilty."

"Don't blame him too much, honey," said Lottie. "Kane was pretty damn well convinced anyhow. If I was in your husband's place and I seen the chance, I'd probably do the same thing."

"I still wish he hadn't done it," said Ellie, "but wishing never got anyone anything. I'll just have to go on from here. Things have got to work out. One way or another, they've got to."

Lottie sighed.

"Give us a cup of coffee, will you, Arch?" she said. "You want a cup of coffee, honey?"

"Yes, thanks," said Ellie.

Arch poured two cups of coffee and set them on the bar.

"Let's go sit down," said Lottie.

The two women took their coffee and moved to a table. Arch stayed behind the bar.

"Have you talked to Denver?" said Ellie, her voice low.

"No," said Lottie. "I haven't seen him since all this happened. It was Kane and some temporary deputies who came in here."

"I wonder how Richard got out?"

"Me, too, but I guess we'll find out soon enough. Are you doing okay? I mean, in your condition and all."

"Oh, yes," said Ellie. "It's still early, I guess. I hardly notice it yet."

"I hate it for you to be going through all this," said Lottie.

"It's nothing to what you've been going through," said Ellie. "For over three months now. We've got to get all this cleared up. And soon."

"Well, we've spread your little rumor around for you. Bonnie let it slip out, you know, to the sheriff's kid. And I said something to Arch. He tells anybody anything. Then there's a fellow comes in here now and then who talks so much we call him Talking Joe. Queenie fed him the whole story."

"Good," said Ellie. "Maybe the killer will be smoked out by the talk."

"Yeah," said Lottie. "God Almighty, honey, that scares me to death. You be damn careful. You hear? Be damn careful."

"Hey, Sheriff. Over here."

"What is it?" said Kane.

"There's a dead man over here."

"Is it Fuller?"

"Nope. It's some stranger, I think."

Kane and the other members of his group rode over to join the man who had made the gruesome discovery. Kane swung down out of the saddle and knelt beside the body of Franklin Smith.

"It's that man that come in on the stage with Mrs. Fuller," he said. "I had a talk with him the other day because he was going around asking questions about them murdered whores."

"Maybe he asked too many questions," said the man who had discovered the body.

"Maybe," said Kane, "or maybe he ran across a man who had just escaped from jail."

"Fuller?" said one of the posse members.

"If he'd bash in one man's brains, he'd shoot another," said Kane. "Fire off three shots."

The sun was almost down when the posse got back to town bringing along the body of Smith.

179

Kane climbed down wearily from the saddle and stepped up on the sidewalk to face his posse.

"Thank you, men," he said. "Those of you with sheriff's department weapons bring them inside and check them in. Aside from that, you're dismissed."

He went into the office, and the man beside Denver Bond leaned over to speak to the deputy in a low voice.

"Denver," he said, "the sheriff said there wasn't no sign out there around that body."

"Yeah," said Bond. "That's why he called off the search."

"There was buggy tracks out there, Denver," said the man. "They led off toward the creek, and then they led back to town. And they went right beside that body."

"They could have been there before the man was killed," said Denver.

"Yeah," said the other man, "or during or after."

"You're right. Just keep it to yourself for now. All right?"

"If you say so."

"I don't know why Ben chose to ignore them tracks, and I don't want to call him on it just yet. We'll see how things develop."

When all the weapons had been checked in and the posse had broken up, Kane dismissed Bond, and the deputy walked over to the Rattlesnake. He found Lottie there with Ellie, and he walked over to the table where they sat. Lottie stood up and put her arms around him.

"I'm glad to see you," she said.

"Please join us," said Ellie.

Bond pulled out a chair and sat down, after Lottie had again taken her seat. He took off his hat and tossed it on an empty chair, and then Lottie noticed the abrasion on his forehead.

"What happened to you?" she said.

"Oh, nothing," said Bond.

"Something happened," said Lottie.

"Did Richard do that to you?" said Ellie.

"No," said Bond. "I asked him to, but he wouldn't do it, so I done it myself."

"What?" said Ellie.

"I think you'd better explain that," said Lottie.

"Well," said Bond, "Richard got the drop on me. I got kind of careless, I guess, and he got my gun and made me unlock the cell. I told him to at least hit me to make it look good for when Ben came back, you know, but he wouldn't do it. So I banged my head against the wall a little. That's all."

"So you—helped him to escape?" said Lottie.

"Well, I guess I did, sort of."

"Where did he go?" said Ellie.

"He's over at my house," said Bond. "He's safe. When we searched the whole town, I was the one who went in my own house. I told him you might be able to sneak over to see him."

"Oh, I want to," said Ellie, "but I don't know if it would be safe. I'd hate to lead the sheriff to him."

"Well," said Bond, "maybe we'll figure out a way."

"You need a drink?" said Lottie.

"Yeah," said Bond, "I could sure use one?"

Lottie waved in the direction of Arch and called out to him.

"Arch," she said, "bring Denver a whiskey, will you?"

"Right away," said Arch. He was busy with a customer at the bar.

"While you're at it," said Lottie, "bring me one, too."

"Denver," said Ellie, "is Sheriff Kane in his office?"

"He was when I left," said Bond.

"I think I'll have one more talk with him," said Ellie. "I just feel like I have to try again. I'm not doing anything else."

"I'll go with you," said Lottie.

"Thanks," said Ellie, "but I think maybe I should go by myself this time. He might be more willing to listen if it doesn't look like we're trying to gang up on him. I'll be back shortly. Will you two be here?"

Lottie looked at Bond.

"Yeah," he said. "We'll be here."

Ellie got up and left the Rattlesnake and walked on down to the sheriff's office. Kane was still there, but he didn't appear to be happy to see her.

"Mrs. Fuller," he said, "I've had a long and tiring day, and it's all because your husband broke out of my jail. He might even have killed another man. I'm not in the mood to listen to you defend him."

"What do you mean he might have killed another man?" said Ellie.

"We went out looking for him, and we found Smith out there. He'd been shot."

"Well, what makes you think that Richard did it?"

"We were tracking him," said Kane, his voice filled with exasperation. "He'd just broke out of jail. He was in jail for killing a man. What do you figure I should think?"

"You know what I think, Sheriff," said Ellie, "and you just told me you didn't want to hear any more about it. I'm sorry to have bothered you. I think I made a mistake by coming in here at all. Good night."

"Wait just a minute," said Kane.

Ellie stopped and turned back around to face him.

"Yes?" she said.

"You made more than one mistake, Mrs. Fuller," said Kane. "You show up here wanting to marry a man I've got in jail for murder. Then you start in telling me I don't know my business. You're going to run your own investigation. Then I hear it around town that you're the sister of Coker Jack. You haven't been telling me everything, have you? Coker Jack and Richard Fuller were friends up north. They were likely partners in a crooked gambling game. And now on top of everything else, Fuller knocks my deputy in the head and breaks out of jail, and then I find another corpse. Now you get on out of here before I decide to lock you up for obstructing justice. And I'll tell you one more time my best advice. Go on back home. Leave Jubilation before it's too late."

"Thank you for the advice, Sheriff," said Ellie. "Good night."

He knew that she would not leave town. He

stared at the door for a moment after she had left. She was stubborn, that one. In spite of all he had said, in spite of his advice and his threats, she would stay and she would keep poking around and asking questions. She was trouble. Nothing but trouble, and something would have to be done about her. Something would have to be done soon. He took out his Colt .45 with the four-inch barrel and checked the load. Yes. He had reloaded it. When? He couldn't remember, but it was loaded. He tucked it back into his holster and buttoned his coat around it. Then he got up and turned out the lamp on his desk, leaving the office in darkness. He walked outside, closed and locked the office door and started walking slowly toward the hotel.

Chapter Nineteen

Ellie was in a huff. No matter what she said to the man, no matter how reasonable her arguments, Kane simply would not listen. Trying to talk to him was like trying to carry on a meaningful conversation with a yearling bull. He had no evidence against Richard. None. When talking to Kane, she had graced his actions by referring to circumstantial evidence, but it wasn't really even that. It was no evidence. The more she thought about it, the more enraged she became. Then some of her anger turned toward Richard. The damn fool, she thought. Kane does have a charge against him now. It's breaking jail. She was only about halfway back to the Rattlesnake when she heard footsteps on the board sidewalk across the street. She was not alarmed. It was still early enough in the evening for people to be out and about, but she glanced in that direction. She saw no one, and the sound of the footsteps had ceased. She walked on. Then she heard them again.

She walked on as if she had not noticed anything out of the ordinary, but she shot a glance in the direction of the sounds. A figure of a man, shadowy in the dim light, moved quickly into a recessed doorway to vanish. Ellie walked on. Just a few steps ahead was the corner of a building. A narrow space separated it from the next building. She looked back toward the dark recess across the street, and she thought that she saw a movement. She pulled open her handbag as she hurried her footsteps. Reaching the corner of the building, she ran the last two steps and ducked around into the dark empty space just as a bullet struck the wall behind her. She pulled the British revolver out of the handbag and pressed herself against the side of the building. Slowly, carefully, she eased herself out just enough to see around the corner. She saw the flash and heard the report of a second shot, and she ducked back again, but just for an instant. The sound had scarcely died away before it was answered by a shot from the Webley in Ellie's hand. She knew that she hit somewhere in the recess. More than that she couldn't tell. She pressed herself against the wall and waited. Then the figure came out of the doorway and ran, but as it ran it fired again in her direction. It turned a corner almost directly across the street from where Ellie stood, and as it did, she fired again.

"Ah."

She heard it scream, and she thought that she could see its left hand reach up to the side of its head. It staggered only slightly to its right, then ran on straight and disappeared.

"Damn it," said Ellie.

She ran across the street to the spot where she had last seen the mysterious figure. It was too dark there between the buildings to look for anything, footprints, evidence of a hit.

"Damn," she said again. Then she heard shouts and hurried footsteps somewhere behind her, and she turned back to face the street. There were several people out on the sidewalks. The gunshots had attracted their attention. Denver Bond was the one running. He was coming toward Ellie.

"Denver," said Ellie.

"Ellie? That you?"

He came closer.

"It's me, all right," said Ellie.

Then Bond saw the pistol in her hand. He pulled out his own revolver.

"What's going on?" he said, and he peered down the dark narrow passageway between the buildings.

"It's over for now," said Ellie. "He's gone, whoever he was."

"What happened?"

"I was on my way back to the Rattlesnake from the sheriff's office," she said. "Someone took a shot at me from over here. I ducked around the corner and shot back. He ran through here to get away. I think I nicked him."

"Well, I'll be damned," said Bond. "Are you all right?"

"I'm fine," said Ellie. "I just wish we could see in here."

"You said he was gone," said Bond.

"Yeah," said Ellie, "but we might see some footprints. Maybe some blood, if I got him good enough."

"Oh, yeah," said Bond. "Well, we can look in the morning when it's light."

"No, let's not wait," said Ellie. "Can't we get a lantern or something?"

"Well, yeah. I guess we could try that."

He looked around. Some of the curious had moved closer and were forming a small crowd in the middle of the street. Bond noticed Lottie among them.

"Lottie," he called, and Lottie came running over to them.

"Ellie," she said, "are you all right, honey?"

"I'm fine, Lottie," said Ellie.

"Lottie," said Bond, "can you find us a lantern? I don't want to leave Ellie standing here alone, and I don't want anyone walking through here until we've had a look."

Lottie looked a little perplexed. She didn't know what was going on, but she sensed a certain amount of urgency. She could ask questions later.

"Sure," she said, and she hurried off. A few of the bolder members of the crowd came closer and started to ask questions, but Bond held them off and kept them at a distance. Pretty soon Lottie was back with a lantern. Bond took it from her and held it a ways into the passageway.

"I don't see anything," he said. "Do you?"

"No," said Ellie. "Let's move on in a ways."

They took a couple of cautious steps, Bond holding the lantern well out ahead.

"Look," he said. "Here's some footprints, all right. But I can't tell nothing about them. They could have been made anytime."

"Yeah," said Ellie, "and they're not clear."

Bond moved the lantern around, then he stepped forward again. There were more footprints, but none of them were clear, and as far as Bond and Ellie could tell, they would not lead them anywhere.

"We'll try again tomorrow," said Bond, "but it don't look to me like we're going to find anything here that'll help. You say you think you nicked him though?"

"He was running away when I fired," said Ellie, "and it seemed like he kind of staggered to his right, and his left hand went up to the side of his head."

"A head wound will be hard to hide," said Bond. "Let's get back to the Rattlesnake. Come on."

"No," said Ellie. "I want to see Richard. Can we go to your house?"

"Well, yeah," said Bond. "I guess so."

"I'll ask Lottie to go with us," said Ellie.

They made their way, a little surreptitiously, to Bond's house, and when they opened the front door and stepped in, Richard Fuller came out of the hallway, gun in hand. He tucked the gun in his waistband and stepped toward Ellie.

189

"Ellie," he said, "I'm glad to see you. I've been about to go crazy here wondering what was going on. I thought I heard some shots just a little while ago."

"That was me," said Ellie. "Someone tried to bushwhack me, but I drove him off."

"Who was it?" said Fuller.

"I couldn't tell."

"But we think she gave him a head wound," said Bond. "We'll find him."

"But who would want to shoot Ellie?"

"Probably whoever it is who's been killing the girls," said Bond.

"Ellie," said Fuller, "I don't like this. I think you ought to go back home where you'll be safe."

"I'm not going without you," she said.

"Ellie," said Fuller, and for the first time he put his arms around her and held her close. Lottie nudged Bond in the ribs.

"Let's go in the kitchen," she said, "and make some coffee or something."

"Huh?" said Bond. "Oh. Yeah. Sure."

Bond and Lottie left the room, and Richard kissed Ellie, tenderly at first, then more passionately.

"I love you," he said. "I really do."

"You sound surprised," said Ellie.

"Well, I am," he said, "in a way. But Ellie, I want you safe. You and the baby. I couldn't stand it if anything happened to you because of me."

"Something's already happened to me because of you," said Ellie.

"Well, yeah, but you know what I mean."

"Yes," she said, "but do you know what I mean? Do you know what's happened to me? I'm not alone anymore. Our lives are no longer separate. They're bound together from now on. I'll say it one more time, Richard I'm not leaving here without you. You're my husband, and we have a child coming, and we're a family. And that's the last word on the subject."

"Then we've got to figure out how to get out," said Richard.

"We're working on that," said Ellie.

She moved across the room and sat down in a chair. From the kitchen, Bond and Lottie could see her. They decided that it was a proper time to return.

"We'll have some coffee in a few minutes," said Lottie.

Everyone found a chair and sat down. They were self-consciously quiet for a moment. Then Richard broke the silence.

"All right," he said. "If you're working on it, what have you got?"

"You mean—evidence?" said Bond.

"Yeah," said Richard. "Let's go over all of it. What have we got? Start at the beginning."

"Well," said Bond, "we got someone in this town who's murdering—."

"Whores," said Lottie.

"He's killed four," said Bond. "We're damn near certain that it's one man. The details of each killing have been the same. And we got no clues on any of them."

"Then we got another murder," said Richard. "The one I was arrested for. Someone clubbed Coker Jack to death."

"That could have been the same killer," said Bond, "or it could be someone else. It was a different kind of crime."

"Then there was poor Mr. Smith," said Ellie.

"Shot three times out on the prairie," said Bond. "Now we could be talking still about one killer or maybe two or even three."

"All right," said Fuller, "add to the list whoever took pot shots at Ellie tonight. Thank God, he missed."

"Okay," said Bond. "It could still all be the same killer, or it could be yet a fourth person. We might be looking for anywhere from one to four men."

"Or women?" said Ellie.

"I never thought of that," said Bond, "but, yeah, I guess so."

There was a pause in the discussion, and Lottie stood up.

"I bet the coffee's made," she said. "Everybody want some?"

No one dissented, so Lottie headed for the kitchen. Bond jumped up from his chair.

"I'll give you a hand," he said, and he followed Lottie out of the room. They soon returned with a tray and distributed coffee all around. Then they settled back down.

"Here's a question," said Fuller. "You say there might be one or there might be four. Are there any reasons for us to think that it might be just one? I mean, is there anything that would tie all of these separate incidents together?"

"Bonnie said that Coker Jack claimed to know the identity of the killer," said Ellie.

"And that man Smith was asking all kinds of questions around town about the murders," said Bond.

"And you tonight, Ellie," said Fuller. "How did it go? Oh, yeah, your brother Coker Jack told you who the killer was. Don't look so surprised. Denver told me this morning."

"Denver!" said Ellie.

"He needed to know," said Denver.

"Well, never mind," she said. "It's too late now. And look what all this means. All of the killings and the attempt on my life are related. There is a common thread. They all have something to do with the original murders—the killings of the girls."

"That's right," said Lottie.

"And there's another thing," said Ellie. "We probably now have our first real piece of physical evidence. The man we're looking for almost certainly has a head wound."

"There may be another clue," said Bond. "Out there where they found Smith, someone had drove a buggy out there and back."

Again there was a long pause. This time Richard Fuller broke the silence.

"So what do we do next?" he asked.

"You don't do anything," said Ellie. "You just stay here out of sight."

"All right," said Fuller. "All right. So what do

you do next?"

"Kane said to just forget them buggy tracks," said Bond, "but I guess what I do next is I check at the stable. If I don't find nothing there, I'll look around at whoever's got buggies around here."

"We were going to check between the buildings again when it's light," said Ellie, "just in case we missed anything."

"Yeah," said Bond.

"And we watch for a man with a head wound," said Lottie. "Right?"

"Right," said Bond. He sighed. "By God, I think we're beginning to make some progress here, finally."

Chapter Twenty

Ben Kane sat alone in his living room. He had been there in the big easy chair all night. When he had come home, he had discovered, not to his surprise, that Donald was out. And Donald had not yet come home. Ordinarily Kane would have been up and finished with his breakfast by this time of morning. He would have been at the office already. Instead he sat there where he had been all night. Part of his left ear was dangling grotesquely, and blood was caked in his hair and on the left side of his neck. His collar and the front of his shirt had been blood-soaked, but the blood was all dried. He had not washed, had not changed clothes. He had gone home, settled in his chair and had not moved since.

He had not moved except to pick up his Bible, and as he sat there alone in the morning hours, he read to himself.

Ye are of your father the devil, and the lusts of your father ye will do. He was a murderer from the beginning, and abode not in the truth, because there is no truth in him. When he speaketh a lie, he speaketh of his own: for he is a liar, and the father of it.

Almost automatically, he turned some pages. And he read again, and he read aloud.

Foolishness is bound in the heart of a child; but the rod of correction shall drive it far from him.

He turned a page and read again.

Withhold not correction from the child: for if thou beatest him with the rod, he shall not die.
Thou shalt beat him with the rod, and shalt deliver his soul from hell.
My son, if thine heart be wise, my heart shall rejoice, even mine.

Again he turned pages, and again he read. But throughout all this reading, his face and his voice were almost expressionless.

The rod and reproof give wisdom: but a child left to himself bringeth his mother to shame.
When the wicked are multiplied, transgression increaseth: but the righteous shall see their fall.
Correct thy son, and he shall give thee rest;

yea, he shall give delight unto thy soul.

His fingers sought yet another passage, but his eyes had roved away from the book and stared without expression at the wall across the room. The fingers stopped, as if they had found the page they wanted, and the lips began to move, yet the eyes still stared at the wall.

And he that curseth his father, or his mother, shall surely be put to death.

The door was opened from the outside, and Kane's eyes rolled lazily to the side to watch as Donald came into the room. The young man's eyes were red and seemed to be set in deep, dark depressions below his forehead. His hair was mussed, and his clothing rumpled. He stopped and looked at his father, surprised to find him sitting up in the house at this hour, astonished at his ghastly appearance. He closed the door and waited for a moment.

"Well?" he said.

"Well—what?" said Kane in a hollow voice.

"Where have I been all night?" said Donald. "What have I been doing? When am I going to grow up? You know. All those questions you always ask."

"I don't care, said Kane. "I won't ask those questions again."

"What's gotten into you, Father?" said Donald, walking over to stand in front of the elder Kane. "Ugh. And what's happened to the side of your head?"

The old man did not answer.

"You really ought to go clean that up," said Donald. "It looks awful."

"It doesn't matter," said Kane.

Donald shrugged and turned to leave the room.

"Well," he said, "if you don't care, I certainly don't. I'm going to bed. It's been a long, long night."

"No," said Kane.

Donald stopped and looked back at his father.

"What?" he said.

"You're not going anywhere. You're going to confess," said Kane.

"Confess? Confess to what? To whom?" said Donald. "Should I confess to you? Have you become the Father Confessor? Just what the hell are you talking about, you old fool?"

"You know," said Kane, standing up to face his son. "You know. Why have I, a lawman, hidden evidence? Suppressed evidence? Even destroyed evidence? Why did I arrest an innocent man? Why did I murder a man and attempt the murder of a young woman? A young woman carrying a child? Why? You know. Confess it."

"You?" said Donald. "You did all that? What are you talking about? You murdered a man? Who? That—that stranger? Smith, was it? You did that? And the woman. I heard all that last night. That was you? Why?"

"For you, Donald," said Kane. "For you. They knew what you've been doing. They were getting too close. They knew. They knew what I've known all along. For awhile I tried to deny it, but I knew. And they knew."

Donald walked a little closer to his father and looked him in the eyes.

"You know?" he said.

"I know," said Kane.

"And you killed Smith to protect me? And the girl. You tried to kill her for the same reason? You?"

"I'm your father, Donald," said Kane. "God forgive me. It's not easy raising a boy without a mother. I tried. When your mother left us, I swore I'd do my best by you. And I tried. I made a promise to God that I'd raise you right. In spite of the kind of woman your mother turned out to be, I swore I'd do my best. And I did try. God knows I tried. But my best just wasn't good enough. I've failed. I've failed miserably with you. But it's not too late. It's never too late in the eyes of God."

"What are you talking about?" said Donald.

"It has to stop, son. It's all over now. It's already gone way too far. It's over for you, and it's over for me. Confess now, and we'll go together."

Donald looked intently at his father. It seemed as if the old man had aged suddenly and remarkably, but that was not all. Something else had happened. Old Kane was crazy. There was something fanatical in his eyes, and to Donald it looked particularly dangerous. He might do anything.

"Where is it we're going?" he said.

"You confess, and then we'll go."

"Where?" said Donald. "Where? Where? Where?"

"We have to pay for what we've done, son. We have to pay for our sins. We have to pay for our failures. We'll turn ourselves over to Denver Bond. The judge will be around before much longer, and we'll just let the law take its natural course and let heaven be our final judge."

Donald could see that there was no arguing with his father, but he had no intention of giving himself up to Denver Bond or to anyone else. He had to think fast.

"Father," said Donald, "I'm afraid. I want to—pray first. Please. I want to pray."

Slowly he turned his back on his father, and he dropped first to one knee, then to the other, and he folded his hands, and he dropped them between his thighs.

"I can't do it," he said. "Help me. Pray for me, Father, so I can confess."

Kane stepped boldly up to Donald's back, and he placed his big hands on his son's shoulders, and he gripped them hard, and the grip shot ripples of pain all the way down Donald's arms.

"Our Father, which art in heaven," intoned the elder Kane, "hallowed be thy name. Thy kingdom come. Thy will be done on earth, as it is in heaven."

Donald slowly loosened his clasped hands and untangled his fingers from each other. His right hand crept upward and underneath his jacket, where his fingers wrapped themselves securely around the haft of a long, thin knife.

"Give us this day our daily bread. And forgive us our debts, as we forgive—."

200

That was Kane's last word, for Donald turned swiftly and thrust upward. The thin blade slid easily under the lower rib on the left side of old Kane's breast. It pierced his heart, and the warm, sticky blood ran freely down the knife and over Donald's hand. It ran down his arm, both inside and outside the sleeve. Donald held the hasp tightly and continued to apply upward pressure, as the surprise on his father's face slowly faded into a blank and stupid expression of nothing. Then the heavy body slumped forward, and Donald moved aside and gave it a shove. He stared at the body, at what had been his father. He remained for a time on his knees, astonished at what he had just done. At last he jerked the knife free and stood up.

"You were right about one thing, old man," said Donald. "It's all over for you. And it's all over for me, too, in this one horse town."

He looked at the bloody knife and at the blood on his own arm. He had to get cleaned up before anyone saw him, and, of course, he had to leave town. He had to leave Jubilation far behind him. But first he had to clean up. He would need money. He knew that. He wondered how much cash the old man had on him. Did he have any stashed in the house? He might have. Donald would have to search. He had to get cleaned up, and he had to find some money. He would have to change his clothes. His clothes. He would have to pack. He would find a suitcase and get packed, and then he would buy a ticket for the stage. When did one leave town? He tried to remember, but he wasn't sure. He hoped it would be soon, but not too soon. He didn't want to miss it. Where would it take him? They went out of town in different directions. He knew that much, but he couldn't recall the times they left, or which ones went in which directions. But it didn't matter really. All that mattered was getting away from Jubilation as quickly as possible and going as far away as possible. Before someone came looking for the old man. Before someone saw him all bloody. Before he was caught and arrested. Before they could kill him.

Denver Bond and Ellie had gone back to the scene of the shooting the night before and checked the passageway between the two buildings once again. Even in the daylight, they found no real clues. The footprints, if they were the footprints of the man who had shot at Ellie, were unclear. There was no blood on the ground, so they couldn't be sure that Ellie's shot had found its mark.

"I still think I hit him," she said.

They had crossed the street and found where one of the attacker's bullets had buried itself in the facade of the butcher shop, and Bond had dug out the lead with his penknife. He studied the little lump of lead, then dropped it into his vest pocket.

"It looks about like the ones they dug out of Smith," he said, "but I can't be sure."

"Well," said Ellie, "I think I'll go over to the

Rattlesnake and see Lottie. I can't think of a thing to do other than watch the sides of men's heads."

"I'm going on down to the stable," said Bond. "Follow up on them buggy tracks I told you about."

"All right, Denver," said Ellie.

When Ellie walked into the Rattlesnake, Lottie was just coming down the stairs. Ellie met her at the bottom of the stairway.

"Good morning, honey," said Lottie.

"Good morning. You just getting up?"

Lottie raised her eyebrows at Ellie.

"Oh," said Ellie. "I mean, have you had your coffee yet?"

"I could use a cup," said Lottie. "Get us a table and I'll fetch the java."

Ellie sat down while Lottie got the coffee and brought it over to the table.

"Here it is," said Lottie. "Hot and black."

"Thank you," said Ellie. "Denver and I have just looked over that area across the street again. Where that man who shot at me ran. We didn't find anymore in the daylight than we had seen last night."

"Where's Denver gone to?" said Lottie.

"He said he was going to the stable to follow up on the buggy tracks," said Ellie.

"What did Ben Kane have to say about someone taking shots at you last night?" said Lottie. "How's he going to brush that one off?"

"I asked Denver," said Ellie, "but he hadn't seen

203

the sheriff yet today."

"Ben's usually the first one at the office," said Lottie.

"Well, apparently he wasn't this morning. I would like to know how he's going to respond to that. He's tried to make it sound like I was either imagining things or making things up ever since the first time I tried to talk to him. Well, there's no way I imagined those shots last night."

"You haven't seen anyone with a bandage on his head, have you?"

"No," said Ellie. She took a sip of coffee, and then she sighed. "I wonder how Richard is doing," she said.

"Didn't you ask Denver?"

"I didn't even think of it. Isn't that stupid? Would anyone think anything about it if they saw you go into Denver's house?"

"Hell, no," said Lottie. "Me and Denver've been the favorite local scandal around town for months now."

"Would you go over and look in on Richard for me? Make sure he's had some coffee. Make sure he's not thinking about doing anything crazy."

"Like leaving the house? Sure, honey. I'll do that. But what are you going to do?"

"I'll go down to the sheriff's office, I think. I want to tell him about last night and see what he has to say."

"Okay," said Lottie. "I'll see you later. Back here?"

"Yes," said Ellie. "Back here. Say in about an hour."

Ellie left the Rattlesnake and walked to the sheriff's office, but she found the door locked. She knew where Denver Bond was, but why was Sheriff Kane not in his office? She stood there on the sidewalk for a moment, her hands on her hips. It was aggravating not to be able to find the sheriff when one needed him. After all, she had been shot at. There had been six murders in Jubilation, and Sheriff Kane had made one arrest, and it had been wrong-headed. Well, she wasn't going to let him sleep late when there was so much to be done. A man was crossing the street a few feet away, and she ran over to stop him.

"Excuse me," she said.

"Yes, ma'am?"

"Can you tell me where Sheriff Kane lives?"

Chapter Twenty-one

"Hell, yes, I remember," said Vile. "Ben Kane took one out yesterday. That one right over there."

Bond looked at the buggy. It had been partly disassembled, and it was apparently being repaired.

"You should have seen it before I washed it," said Vile. "The damn thing was covered with mud. Singletree's broke. 'Send me the bill,' he said. That's all. No explanation. No apology. 'Send me the bill.'"

"Thanks, Giff," said Bond. He walked out of the stable and stood for a moment thinking. Kane had said to ignore the tracks. Why? And Kane himself had taken out a buggy that day. Could the tracks that led to the body of Smith and back to town have been made by the same buggy that Kane had used? If so, why didn't he say so? It didn't make sense. Bond decided that he needed someone to talk to about this new development. He walked to the Rattlesnake and found Bonnie and Queenie there together.

"Hi," he said. "Have y'all seen Lottie or Ellie in here?"

"Lottie was just leaving when I come down," said Bonnie. "She said she was going over to your house."

"Thanks," he said.

"Have fun," said Queenie, as Bond was on his way out the door.

Donald had not yet washed the blood off his hand and arm, and he had not yet changed his clothes. He had searched his father's pockets and emptied them of all the money he had found, but it was not enough. He was searching the rest of the house. He was pulling out desk drawers when he saw the motion outside, and he looked up and out the window. He saw Ellie Fuller walking toward the house.

"What?" he said out loud. "What does she want here? Does she know? She knows. Father said she knows. That's why he shot at her. She knows."

He thought of running, but he rejected that as a bad plan. Where would he run to? People would see him with the blood still on his arm. He looked at the knife where he had dropped it on the floor, and he ran to pick it up. The haft was sticky in his hand, and he dropped it again.

"No," he said. "Not that."

He ran to the front door and took hold of the handle. Slowly, easily, he opened the door, but just a crack. Then he stepped behind it. He waited until he heard her footsteps on the porch. Then he heard her knock.

"Sheriff," she called out. "Are you at home? This is Ellie Fuller, Sheriff. Are you in there?"

She knocked again, but this time, instead of knocking on the door frame, she knocked on the door itself, and it swung inward. He waited.

"Sheriff?" she said. "Sheriff Kane?"

He watched as the door swung farther into the room, and then she did what he expected her to do. She stepped inside. One more step, he thought, just one more. She took it, and he grabbed her from behind. His left arm encircled her body, and his right hand, still sticky, with the blood of his father, covered her mouth. She tried to yell, but the sound was muffled. She saw the body on the floor, and she saw its one ragged ear. She struggled, but to no avail. Whoever it was had her in a firm grip.

Bond found Lottie and Richard Fuller drinking coffee in his living room. When he walked in, Lottie jumped up to meet him. He put his arms around her for a moment. Then he released her and went to a chair.

"Can I have some of that?" he said.

"Sure," said Lottie. "I'll get it for you."

She brought him a cup of coffee and then sat back down.

"I just found out something real strange," said Bond.

"Well," said Lottie, "what is it?"

"Remember I told you that there were buggy tracks out where Smith's body was found?"

"Yeah," said Lottie.

"And that Kane had said to ignore them," said

Fuller.

"That's right," said Bond. "I just come from the stable. Giff Vile has buggies to rent out down there. He said Ben Kane took one out yesterday, and Ben brought it back all messed up."

"You think that Kane made those tracks?" said Fuller.

"Well," said Bond, "it sounds that way. Don't it? But why didn't he tell me? Why did he just say to ignore them?"

"Maybe he didn't want you to know he'd been out there," said Lottie. "Maybe—."

She stopped when she realized what it was she was about to say. She looked at Bond, and he stared back at her.

"Maybe Ben Kane killed Smith," said Fuller. "Is that what you were about to say?"

"I—yeah," said Lottie. "I think that is what I was going to say."

"No," said Bond. "I can't believe that. Why would Ben kill that guy? It don't make any sense."

"It's the only thing that does make sense," said Fuller. "Finally something makes sense. Come on. Think it all through. Kane was after me for killing Coker Jack right from the first. For no reason. Then he arrested me without any evidence. And he wouldn't listen to anyone. Not me, not Ellie, not you. Then when you find another body, and you find a real clue, he says to ignore it. Come on, Denver. He's our killer."

"But those girls?" said Bond.

"I don't know about that," said Fuller. "Let's take one thing at a time. Sheriff Ben Kane killed Coker Jack and Smith. Have you seen Kane today?"

"No," said Bond. "He didn't come into the office this morning."

"See?" said Fuller.

"See what?"

"Whoever shot at Ellie last night got a head wound. Right? If Kane showed himself today, he'd give himself away. He's hiding."

"That might explain something else," said Bond.

"What?" said Lottie.

"Why he didn't hit Ellie last night," said Bond. "Ben carries that short-barreled Colt. He couldn't hit anything at that distance."

"Well, what do we do, Denver?" said Lottie.

"I—I don't know," said Bond. "Wait a minute. Let me think."

"What's there to think about?" said Fuller. "When the sheriff goes bad, the deputy has to take over."

"He took the buggy out," said Lottie.

"And he told you to ignore the tracks," said Fuller. "You've got more on him than he had on me, and he threw me in jail."

"You're right," said Bond. "If this doesn't work, I'm out of a job, but, what the hell? Let's go."

She was tied to the chair so tightly that she couldn't move, and she couldn't scream or shout because of the rag tied around her mouth. She wondered why he hadn't just killed her, the way he had killed so many others, Georgia and Mary and Bridgit and Lola and his own father. She didn't know about Coker Jack and Smith, but she felt certain that either Donald or Ben Kane had killed those two. She knew that it had been the sheriff who shot at her, for she could see him lying dead there on the floor, and she could see his mangled left ear where her bullet had torn it. Donald had tied her to the chair, and then he had gone into another room. She wondered what he was up to. She wondered what he had planned for her.

When he came back into the living room, he had washed his hands. He had also changed his clothes, and he was carrying a suitcase. He paused in the middle of the room, and he looked at Ellie there in the chair, and he smiled. He put the suitcase down by the door, and then he noticed her handbag where she had dropped it. He picked it up and opened it.

"Oh, my," he said, and he removed the Webley, holding it between his thumb and forefinger. He dropped it on the floor. He stepped over to a table and emptied the contents of the purse out, picking out all the money, which he then stuffed into his pockets.

"Every little bit counts," he said. Then he walked over to stand in front of Ellie. He leaned down toward her, and he looked into her eyes. "I'm leaving now," he said. "It's all over here. I have to go away."

He straightened up again, reached into a pocket and pulled out a wooden match, which he held up for Ellie to see. "This old house will go up in no time," he said. "You won't suffer long. The stagecoach is just about ready to leave, and by the time this has burned out and they discover bodies in here, I'll be long gone. It's perfect."

He smiled again, and walked over to the desk which stood beneath the window. On the top of the desk was a disarray of papers. He shoved them toward the back of the desk, wadded a few sheets up, and struck the match. He lit a sheet of paper on fire and dropped it back onto the other papers. Flames reached up toward the flimsy curtain which hung down from the window. Soon the curtain was a-flame. Donald took three quick steps to the door, picked up his suitcase and was gone.

Ellie struggled, but she could not get loose. She tried making the chair walk across the room by rocking back and forth, but she almost capsized, so she quit. She didn't want to be lying helpless on the floor. If she could only scream to get someone's attention, she thought, and she tried to bite at the gag with her teeth, but she had no luck there. Her only hope was that someone would see the smoke before the fire got to her. At least, it seemed to be her only hope.

Bond tried the door to the sheriff's office and found it locked.

"He ain't been here yet," he said.

"What did I tell you, Denver?" said Fuller. "He's hiding out."

"Come on," said Bond.

"Where we going?" said Fuller.

"Kane's house. Come on."

Bond started down the street at a trot, and Fuller and Lottie both followed. Just then Donald Kane stepped around the corner. He was startled to see the three running toward him. Bond stopped.

"Donald," he said, "is your old man at home?"

"Yes," said Donald. He answered quickly and sharply.

"Thanks," said Bond. Then he noticed Donald's suitcase. "You going somewhere?" he said.

"I'm going back to Austin," said Donald, "back to finish college. Father's been trying to get me to go back for some time now. I just decided that now is the time to do it. He's right."

"I don't suppose you've seen my wife," said Fuller.

"Your wife?"

"You know who she is," said Bond. "They were married at the jail."

"Oh, yes," said Donald. "Yes. She came to the house. She wanted to talk to my father."

"Is she still there?" said Fuller.

"Look," Donald shouted, and he pointed at the same time. "Smoke. Something's on fire over there."

"My God, it is," said Bond.

"My house is over that way," said Donald.

"Come on," said Bond, and he started running, but Donald ran in the opposite direction. Fuller and Lottie ran after Bond. It was several blocks to the Kane house by the streets, but Bond knew where he was going. He cut across fields and ran through yards. When they reached the house, they were panting for breath, and the front wall of the house was almost consumed by the flames.

"God," said Bond, "the whole house will go up in no time."

"Ellie," said Fuller, and he ran toward the flames, but the heat drove him back.

"You can't go in there," said Bond.

"Try the back," said Lottie.

They ran around the house, heading for the back, but on the way, Fuller noticed that the side wall was not yet on fire except toward the front. He ran up to a side window and looked in.

"She's in there," he yelled. He tried to raise the window, but it was latched on the inside. Bond had run on around to the back of the house where he found the back door unlocked. He went inside, choking on the smoke that had already filled the small house. He made his way quickly into the living room, and there he saw Ellie. He also saw the body of Ben Kane, but he didn't have time to worry about that. He grabbed the chair back to which Ellie was tied and began dragging the chair across the floor. Fuller was still standing outside the window. Bond grabbed up a small table and shouted at the top of his voice.

"Get back," he said.

When Fuller saw Bond raise the table, he jumped out of the way, and Bond smashed the window, then quickly raked a table leg across the window sill to knock away bits of broken glass. He tossed the table aside and went back to Ellie, dragging the chair up to the window. Richard reached in from the outside to help, and the two men together managed to get the chair with Ellie still tied to it out through the window. Richard dragged Ellie farther from the burning house, while Bond climbed out the window. As soon as they were a safe distance from the house, Lottie untied the gag that had kept Ellie quiet. With the gag off, Ellie began to cough. Richard untied the ropes that bound her to the chair, and she stood up and looked at the flames licking their way around the house.

"God," she said.

Richard put his arms around her.

"Ellie," he said. "Oh, Ellie. Are you all right?"

"Yes," she said. "I am now. Thanks to you and Denver. And you, Lottie. Kane is in there. He's dead."

"I saw him," said Bond.

"He was the one who shot at me," said Ellie. "I saw his ear. My bullet tore his ear."

"So it was Ben," said Bond, "but then, who killed Ben?"

"Donald," said Ellie, "and it was Donald who tied me to the chair and set fire to the house. He said he was leaving, and he took a suitcase."

"That's right," said Lottie. "We saw him with a suitcase."

"You two stay with Ellie," said Bond. "I'm going after Donald."

Bond turned and ran back toward the main part of town. Ellie took a few more deep breaths.

"But why would Donald kill his father?" said Lottie.

"I'll tell you what I think," said Ellie. "I think Donald was the killer, and I think that his father knew all along. I think that Ben Kane killed Smith and shot at me trying to protect Donald."

"What about Coker Jack?" said Richard.

"I don't know which of the two killed him," said Ellie, "but Coker Jack had bragged that he knew the identity of the killer. If Donald didn't kill him to protect himself, then Ben did it for the same

215

reason."

"Then it was Donald who killed all the girls," said Lottie. "It was Donald all along. Denver's got to catch him."

"Let's go make sure," said Ellie.

"Are you sure you ought to—?" Lottie began.

"Come on," said Ellie. "I'm all right."

Chapter Twenty-two

Donald ran into the stage depot. His hands fumbled as he dug into his pockets for money to pay his fare. He was nervous. It was rotten luck to have run into Bond like that. He had hoped that they wouldn't notice the smoke quite so soon, and then he, himself, in order to get rid of them, had pointed it out. He had panicked. Well, he thought, maybe they'd be busy fighting the fire long enough for him to get safely out of town yet. The fire should occupy all their attention for awhile yet, and the stagecoach was sitting in the street in front of the station ready to go. Still he was nervous. He hurried back out to the stage. The driver took his suitcase and stowed it in the back boot.

"When do we leave?" asked Donald.

"About thirty minutes," said the driver. "Don't go off too far."

"Thirty minutes?" said Donald. "No sooner?"

"Nope."

Donald looked nervously down the street. He wondered where he could hide for thirty minutes and still get back in time to catch the stage out of town. Would the fire keep the others busy that long? Thirty minutes. He was afraid that it would not. Would they discover the bodies before then and come looking for him? He thought about going to the stable to get his father's horse, but he hated horses, and he had never been able to handle them well. He could get a buggy, he thought. He could drive a buggy. He turned to head for the stable. Then he saw Denver Bond coming toward him. He couldn't tell if Bond had seen him or not. The deputy might just have been headed for the station. Donald walked around the front of the stage, going all the way in front of the lead horses. Then he started to cross the street. Bond spotted him and started to run. Donald ran. He ran up onto the sidewalk, and he ran into a man who was walking in the opposite direction.

"Hey," said the offended man. "Watch where the hell you're going."

Donald ran, and people on the sidewalk got out of his way. He looked over his shoulder, and he could see Bond coming after him. He turned his head forward so he could see where he was going, and then he saw Richard Fuller coming from the other direction. He darted between two buildings. Bond saw him and gestured to Fuller to circle around. Fuller turned a corner, and so did Bond. When Donald ran out from between the two buildings, he saw the two men come around corners, one on each side of him. He stopped and turned, running back between the same two buildings, retracing his own steps. This time he ran to the middle of the street and headed out of town. He ran as fast as he could, and he beat Bond. He ran past the stagecoach. Bond was behind him, and Fuller was even farther behind. Donald was almost out of town, headed for the open prairie. He had only to pass by Grover's Farm Implement Store and Kelley's Billiard Hall, and he would be out of town.

He wondered if Bond and Fuller would continue to run after him. It occurred to him that they might give up and get themselves some horses and come after him that way. But by the time they had done all that, he could be hiding somewhere. It was too much to think about. He was running, and he had to get away. He passed by the Farm Implement Store, and then he saw the others coming toward him from out on the prairie. There were two men on horseback, and one of the men was leading a horse with a saddle but no rider. He didn't recognize the men, could not even see them clearly, but he felt as if people were coming at him from all directions. He stopped and turned again. There was no place else to go. He ran back toward the stage station, and there was Ellie. She should have burned up. She was standing beside the stagecoach with a pistol in her hand.

"Give up, Donald," she said.

He was just in front of the Farm Implement Store, and he turned again, but his foot slipped in the loose dirt, and he fell. He was falling backward, and he turned as he fell in an attempt to break his fall with his hands. Too late he saw the shining, new Keystone disc-harrow proudly displayed there in the street in front of Grover's Farm Implements. He started to scream as he fell toward the sharp discs, and he tried to turn aside as he fell, but all too late. The last disc on the right-hand gang sliced his neck as he fell. His neck was cut half in two on the right side. He fell on his face, and his body gave one last spasm. Then he lay still in an expanding dark pool of blood.

Richard Fuller was the first to reach the body. He stopped and stared in disbelief. He was soon joined by Bond, and then by Ellie. By the time Lottie reached the scene, a small crowd had gathered there around the gruesome sight. Fuller put an arm around Ellie. She turned her face away from the spectacle and buried it in Richard's chest. Bond put an arm around Lottie, but Lottie continued to stare at the body with hatred in her eyes. Others in the crowd began asking questions. What was going on here? That was Donald Kane, the sheriff's boy. What was the gambler doing out of jail? Did the others in the crowd know that the sheriff's house had just burned down? Where was the sheriff, anyhow? Bond finally hushed the crowd. He stepped up on a box there in front of Grover's store.

"I'll give y'all a quick explanation," he said, "and then I want you to break it up and go on about your business."

J.W. McKee and Sandy rode up behind the crowd. They sat there in their saddles, listening to the deputy's speech.

"Now, I ain't going to try to tell y'all how we come to figure this all out," said Bond. "I'm just going to tell you what we know. Donald Kane was the one who killed them four girls."

There were mumblings in the crowd, but they soon quieted down. Everyone wanted to hear everything that Bond would have to say.

"Old Ben Kane," Bond continued, "he found out, and he done some bad things to cover up for his boy. Y'all might have heard already that Coker Jack had spouted off that he knew who the killer was. Well, you know what happened to him. He was beat to death. It might have been Donald that done it, or it might have been Ben. We don't know that one for sure, but we do know that Ben tried to blame it on Richard Fuller, here."

J.W. shot a glance at Sandy.

"He went so far as to arrest Fuller and throw him in jail. Y'all know that part. Then that fellow Smith come into town and started asking all kinds of questions about the murders, and Ben took him out of town and shot him dead. We know that. Then Ben tried to kill Mrs. Fuller, but she outdone him. She shot back and nicked his ear, and he run off. Then something happened between Ben and Donald, and Donald killed his daddy. He set fire to the house. Anyway, that's all y'all need to know for now, and it's all over and done with. Now, I'd appreciate it if you'd break it up, and let us get things cleaned up here."

Bond dropped down off the box, and the crowd slowly dispersed. Bond asked one of the men to fetch Mort Sexton. But the two men on horseback stayed. Bond was just about to accost them and ask them what their business was in Jubilation, but he noticed that they were staring hard at the backs of Ellie and Richard. One of them, the oldest, spoke before Bond had made up his mind what to say.

"Mr. Fuller," said the old-timer, "I had first thought to kill you when I found you."

Fuller and Ellie turned around to face the new voice.

"Daddy," said Ellie.

"Like I said, Mr. Fuller," J.W. continued, "my first thought was to kill you. Then when I'd had time to reflect a little, I thought that I might horsewhip you first, and then kill you. Well, I've had a letter from my daughter since then, and I've had a long ride,

221

and I've changed my mind."

"I'm glad of that, Mr. McKee," said Fuller. "And what, may I ask, have you finally settled on?"

"Something that's probably worse than horsewhipping or killing, for you."

"Daddy," said Ellie, her voice pleading.

"First I have to ask you a question," said J.W.

"All right," said Fuller.

"Am I correct in assuming that the lady standing beside you is Mrs. Fuller?"

"That is correct, sir," said Fuller. "Now may I hear your decision regarding my—fate worse than death?"

"I'm taking you back to the ranch with me and putting you to work," said J.W. "If you don't like the idea, I can always go back to my first plan."

"I like it very much, Mr. McKee," said Fuller. "That is, if Ellie agrees."

J.W. looked down into his daughter's face for the first time.

"Well?" he said. "Do you agree?"

"Yes, Daddy," said Ellie. "Of course, I agree. Thank you."

J.W. swung down wearily from the saddle, and Sandy followed suit. The foreman took the reins of J.W.'s horse. J.W. walked over to Ellie and Fuller. He reached out for Fuller's hand.

"Your my daughter's husband," he said, "and you're going to be the father of my grandchild. The past is forgot. Welcome to the family."

"Thank you, sir," said Fuller.

"Call me J.W. Have you met my foreman?"

"No, sir, J.W.," said Fuller. "I haven't."

"This is Sandy MacColl," said J.W. "Sandy, this is my son-in-law, Richard Fuller."

"Hello, Sandy," said Richard.

222

"Howdy," said Sandy.

Ellie walked over close to Sandy and hugged him.

"Sandy," she said, "thanks for coming with him. And you brought Sampson."

"Yes, ma'am," said Sandy.

"I'm so glad to see him. Thank you. Thank you, Daddy."

Mort Sexton came driving up in his wagon, and Bond went to meet him. He pointed toward the body there beside the disc-harrow.

"Mort," he said, "would you take care of this?"

Sexton nodded solemnly and went to work.

"Well," said J.W., "Sandy and I have had a long ride. Do you think we could find a good meal and then a place to spend the night?"

"Of course," said Ellie. "But I have some new friends I'd like for you to meet. Could they join us?"

"Sure," said J.W.

"This is Denver Bond," said Ellie. "He's the deputy sheriff here, and he's been a great help to us. And this is Lottie, she's his — ."

"Fiancee," said Lottie, and she glanced at Bond to see how he would react to that astonishing announcement. He appeared to be awestruck, but he moved quickly to her side and took her hand in his.

"Yes," he said. "We're very happy to meet you, Mr. McKee. Your daughter has become a good friend to us."

"The best," said Lottie.

"So you're the local law?" said J.W. as he shook Bond by the hand.

"Well, yes, sir," said Bond. "What's left of it. For now anyway. I think that I'll quit, and me and Lottie will try to find someplace to start over."

He was speaking to J.W., but he was looking at

223

Lottie. Her face told him that she liked that idea.

"Well," said J.W., "if you four have got to be such good friends, and if you two plan to leave here anyway, why don't you just go home with us? How do you feel about ranch work, Mr. Bond?"

"Why, hell, sir," said Bond. "That's what I used to do before I put on this badge. I'd be real grateful. Lottie?"

"Yes," said Lottie. "Let's do it."

Ellie stepped up to her father and reached around his neck and smiled into his weathered old face.

"Daddy," she said, "I love you."

"There's one other thing we have to take care of," said J.W.

"What's that, Daddy?"

"We have to find a telegraph office and send your mother word that everything has turned out just fine, and that we'll all be home together real soon."